TRUTH AND CONSEQUENCE

Helen's trust in her older husband Paul is shaken when a letter arrives from a man claiming to be his son. The charming Simon visits and immediately challenges Helen's martial contentment. She succumbs to his advances unaware they're made from a desire for vengeance. Helen guiltily turns her back to Paul as Simon realizes he loves her but she might never trust him. Deeply depressed, Paul attacks his son bringing a final end to his marriage. Helen leaves with Simon and they all find a way to live with the consequences of the past while moving forward with their new lives.

Truth And Consequence

by

Angela Britnell

Dales Large Print Books
Long Preston, North Yorkshire,
BD23 4ND, England.

British Library Cataloguing in Publication Data.

Britnell, Angela
    Truth and consequence.

A catalogue record of this book is
available from the British Library

ISBN   978-1-84262-874-4 pbk

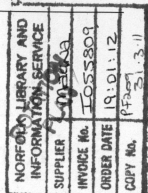

Cover illustration © Stephen Carroll by arrangement with
Arcangel Images

The moral right of the author has been asserted

Published in Large Print 2012 by arrangement with
Angela Britnell

Dales Large Print is an imprint of Library Magna Books Ltd.

Printed and bound in Great Britain by
T.J. (International) Ltd., Cornwall, PL28 8RW

CHAPTER ONE

'The cruellest lies are often told in silence.'
Robert Louis Stevenson

The cheap white envelope lay innocuously between the marmalade pot and the glass butter dish exactly where Helen had placed it after sorting the post. If Paul had looked he might have recognized the handwriting, even after nearly thirty years. Instead he was concentrating on reading the local paper, frowning over the top of his glasses at the news that a by-pass was finally going to be built around Carveth.

Rain misted up the windows but still Helen went back to gazing at the group of people huddled under their umbrellas at the bus stop. They looked fed up which didn't stop her feeling a little niggle of envy. She told herself that most of them were probably going to do extremely boring jobs for eight hours, wouldn't be paid much and the women especially had to come home afterwards and start working all over again. But still...

Paul gave his wife's arm a gentle nudge. 'Could you pour me some more tea if

5

you've finished daydreaming?' His voice startled her. Recently it had become harder to concentrate, with her mind frequently drifting off somewhere without her.

Helen picked up the pot and fixed Paul's tea with plenty of milk and two sugars before refilling her own cup. She made it black with no sugar because it *had* been a struggle, yet again, to do up the top button of her jeans earlier. It would doubtless sit there not drunk but at least she'd feel somewhat virtuous.

'So where had you wandered off to?' Worry darkened his eyes to almost a navy blue. Helen briefly considered the truth. Only briefly though. She responded gently that it was nowhere exciting and the reassurance removed a few of the grey shadows from his skin. Paul didn't deserve a bad start to his week after being up half the night delivering Mattie Truscott's latest baby. In an ideal world he'd be able to go back to bed and rest but that would make a waiting room of patients at the surgery very unhappy. His weariness reminded Helen that Paul was nearly fifty, something she often forgot, the increasing streaks of grey threading through his once black hair merely an extra confirmation.

He persisted as if needing convincing, 'You wouldn't rather be heading off to do eight hours in the exciting building society I rescued you from?' His loving smile lifted her heart at the same time as it lightened the tiredness in his own face. 'What do you think?' It wasn't hard to be less than honest if you loved someone enough.

'I think you're a lovely woman and a saint especially as I know you'll get the brunt of Mother's bad temper later. She was in the kitchen when I got back earlier moaning about not sleeping well last night.' That sounded pretty normal to Helen. For the six long years since Alice's stroke she'd struggled to be patient – putting up with her mother-in-law's constant complaints about something or somebody.

He popped a kiss on the top of her head and turned back to the newspaper. Helen checked through the rest of the post first tossing to one side the useless adverts for storm windows and alarm systems. There was the bill for the new curtains, time enough to share quite how much they'd ended up costing when the bank statement arrived. Still the way the green and cream Liberty print matched the carpet perfectly was very satisfying.

Idly rubbing at the sticky blob of orange marmalade she'd dropped on the white cloth Helen wondered whether she'd get away by covering it with a vegetable dish at dinnertime tonight. Pushing a few stray soft brown curls back away from her face she got up and began to pile the dishes onto a tray.

Afterwards Helen wasn't sure which she'd heard first, Paul's sharp intake of breath or the noise of his knife clattering suddenly onto the plate. Whichever it was made her turn to look.

He hadn't paid any attention to the envelope merely opening it absentmindedly while thinking about Tom Harris, his first patient. It never got any easier to have to tell someone there was really nothing to be done. It was only when he finally looked properly at the single sheet of paper he'd taken out that he realized.

For a fleeting moment Helen had the ridiculous idea his hands were shaking. He'd certainly gone very pale and was staring at the letter in what looked almost like disbelief.

'What is it? Let me see.'

As she reached to take it Paul quickly pushed the letter back into the envelope. 'It's nothing important. Look I've got to be going darling. The surgery meeting's due to start in ten minutes and you know how annoyed James gets if anyone's late. I'll see you at lunchtime.' Before she could consider saying anything else he'd picked up his bag and left, not even stopping to collect his raincoat or an umbrella. Their usual goodbye kiss was overlooked.

No doubt it was one of those nasty chain letters that he didn't want her to worry about. He was always sweet about protecting her from upsets. Helen's mind swiftly moved on as she headed for the kitchen thinking of the list of jobs to be worked through before the day finished.

Measuring the usual amount of flour into her mother's old white bowl Helen smiled inwardly as she ran a finger along the snake like crack running up one side. Helen's mother had shared with her how she'd dropped the bowl in shock as her first labour pang hit. The grainy soft powder ran through her fingers and with the yeast already bubbling away nicely in the warm water she quickly made up the dough, slapped it down on the old pine table and kneaded it into a smooth ball. That erased the last of the lingering discontent – bread making was good for that. Covered with a clean tea towel the bowl was placed on the Aga, in exactly the right spot for it to rise – not too hot and not too cold, rather like Baby Bear's porridge.

Carelessly wiping floury hands on her old jeans she gazed contentedly around the room. Thank goodness the nasty green lino on the floor and dark brown paint that had made it resemble a train station waiting room was gone. Alice hadn't understood why it had been the first thing to be changed when handing over the house to her newly married son ten years ago. Now Helen could work surrounded by cheery yellow walls, pale grey cupboards, and the brightly painted pottery bought on their honeymoon in Sorrento. It didn't look as though they'd get back there any time soon so this was the next best thing.

The clock chimed ten thirty. Helen swiftly laid a tray with Alice's treasured Royal Worcester china. If she hadn't spent yesterday afternoon reading her library book the choice now wouldn't be creased linen napkins or paper. Two of the cheap blue paper ones picked up at the market last Thursday would have to do. Of course Alice would notice and naturally wouldn't attempt to hide her distaste, anything less than starched linen was considered bad manners. Thank goodness at least Paul's father, Jack, wouldn't care. His sweet nature often saved her sanity.

Helen made the coffee, tidied her hair, put on some cheerful pink lipstick and set off with a little smile tugging at the corners of her mouth remembering her friend Julie calling Alice's room 'the dragon's lair.' Helen wasn't in the mood for fire-breathing this morning.

CHAPTER TWO

*'No one can make you feel inferior without
your consent.'*
Eleanor Roosevelt

Before opening the door Helen took a deep
breath and fixed on the expected concerned
smile. The stifling heat mixed the aromas of
mothballs, lavender water and last night's
fish pie together unpleasantly in her nostrils.
It wasn't easy but she managed to find a
space for the tray on the only spare corner
of an already over burdened table.

The room was crammed with Alice's
favourite pieces of dark Victorian furniture
collected from around the house. It was
amusing how she believed she'd put one
over on her daughter-in-law by squirrelling
away the 'best' things whereas Helen was
only too relieved not to have to live with the
gloomy stuff. Commemorative royal mugs,
silver framed photos of long dead relatives
and scores of miniature china cups jostled
for the small pools of available space left.

Alice had manoeuvred her wheelchair over
to the bay window as usual and was busily
scrutinizing everything going on in the street.

While she watched her hands continuously worked a sharp needle in and out of yet another one of the religious embroideries she so loved. Helen had last year's Christmas present with its unsubtle reference to 'Honour thy father and thy mother' stuffed in the back of her wardrobe.

'Sorry I'm a bit late, Jack. There's your coffee. Would you like some shortbread?' Folding the newspaper he tucked it down on the floor by his worn plaid slippers before taking his cup from Helen's outstretched hand. The watery sunlight emphasized his pale stretched out old man's skin. As always he smiled kindly and thanked her.

'Left from yesterday I suppose? I'll have a small piece seeing as there's nothing else on offer.' Alice's bitterness cut scathingly through her husband's generosity. Helen sympathized with how much she resented having to rely on them all but some days it was harder than others to be tolerant and this was definitely one of those days. Instead of stopping to chat it was wiser to leave now and hope that lunchtime would be an improvement. Alice was always more circumspect when Paul was around. Helen made it halfway out the door before the first dart struck.

'I do hope Sarah's letter didn't cause any trouble this morning dear?'

Helen bit down hard on her lip to stifle a hasty reply. She hated the spiteful inference that Alice knew something she herself didn't. It was a struggle to make her face reflect indifference while selecting her words with excruciating care. 'Oh, of course not Alice. There's absolutely no reason for it to.'

The older woman's silence was smug. Helen hadn't fooled her. They both knew that.

Somehow her legs got her back to the kitchen and gratefully into the nearest chair. Who the hell was Sarah anyway? She didn't know what to think. Picking up the phone she dialled Julie's number, her usual automatic reaction. There were ten long rings before Roger's harsh voice barked out a rough, 'Yes.'

Red. That was the colour she associated with Roger. Years ago it was his flashy sports car but now it was his face, habitually flushed with anger and alcohol. Julie always quietly ignored Helen's hinted questions by changing the conversation. Still the unexplained bruises darkening her friend's slim arms when the summer heat drove her into short sleeves and the way Livvy and John sheltered by their mother only made Helen certain of her fears.

One night in bed Helen had hinted to Paul that all might not be well with their friends but unusually he'd mocked her. His words had hurt. 'Oh Helen sweetie, you've been doing one of those stupid magazine quizzes again haven't you? What is it this time? Ten ways to recognize domestic violence? Go to sleep dear.' After all these years she should have known better than to criticize Roger seeing the two men had been friends since being thrown into the lion's den of boarding school as scared eight year olds. Their loyalty wasn't negotiable. The suggestion had never been mentioned again.

'Julie's out.' Roger's sharp voice defied questions so Helen hung up. The grandfather clock in the hall struck eleven meaning if she didn't go soon and buy a few things for lunch she'd only get further behind. Helen pulled on her old gardening coat and went off down the street.

The early morning's heavy drizzle had worsened to a steady penetrating rain. It forced Helen to put on the old scarf she kept in the pocket. She detested the things really, considering them on a level with plastic rain hats, and had sworn to her mother never to wear one but it was that or wet frizzy hair.

Bending to avoid the low doorway Helen stepped down into the shop and made her way through the overcrowded aisles. Picking up a plastic-wrapped wedge of cheddar, some rather orange looking tomatoes and two pints of semi-skimmed milk she straightened herself, physically and mentally, to face Emily Grant standing guard over the till.

A clear snapshot of herself as a scared five-year-old, unkindly berated for not having enough money to buy the loaf of bread her mother had sent her for, flashed in front of her eyes. The thin, drawn unsmiling woman measuring out small bags of fresh yeast hadn't changed much in those thirty years; she still wore a practical dark Crimplene dress every day covered up with a brown apron. Her legs were encased in thick stockings finished off with sensible flat lace-up shoes. Her voice remained sharp as vinegar and her words equally acid.

'Good morning, Mrs. Barton.' Funny how as soon as she married and became a doctor's wife that had made it somehow improper for Emily Grant to use her first name. 'Late today aren't we?' One day Helen swore she'd be able to overcome her habitual well-mannered quietness and answer back but it wouldn't be this particular morning.

The woman's hands, clawed with rheumatism, placed each item slowly into a flimsy plastic bag, the handles of which would probably break before Helen got home. There was something suspiciously resembling a smile hovering around Mrs. Grant's pursed lips. It was a rare and not particularly pretty sight.

'I helped out a young man earlier who was looking for your husband, Mrs. Barton.' Her dark narrow eyes fixed on Helen made her understand what a struggling butterfly skewered on a board must feel like. She couldn't even pinpoint why she felt so uneasy. People were always asking for directions to the surgery so what was so interesting about that? Helen dragged out a polite smile and thanked the woman, presuming that was what was required.

'Had long hair he did and one of those big backpacks.' Helen had no idea what more she was expected to say. 'I suppose he must have been a new patient, Mrs. Grant.' The older woman's face twisted into a silent sneer. Taking her bag Helen left.

Emily Grant knew more than she was letting on but what about Helen didn't have a clue. The uncomfortable chill deep inside her had nothing to do with the weather.

CHAPTER THREE

'The truth is rarely pure and never simple.'
Oscar Wilde

Helen dragged ineffectually at the sleeves of her soaking wet mac as the phone rang. Naturally it stopped as soon as she managed to get her second arm out. The only things handy to replace her soggy shoes were the ugly fuzzy blue slippers Alice and Jack had given her for her birthday. She hated the way they made her already large feet look even bigger.

Before grating the cheese Helen roughly pulled her hair back out of the way with a rubber band. It wasn't the time to fuss about split ends. The relentlessly dreary day was getting to her so she laid the table with her favourite red and yellow Italian plates. Maybe changing into the red T-shirt Julie had persuaded her to buy in Plymouth would be a good idea too. Anything to lift this awful feeling of something being very wrong.

She wished she could stop her mind going over and over Alice's comment. Maybe this Sarah was an old girlfriend? It wasn't something she and Paul had ever found much of a need to talk about. Alice took every opportunity to put her down – she should know that by now. It would prove to be a lot of fuss over nothing.

Helen lifted the bubbling dish of macaroni cheese out on top of the Aga to keep warm and its rich heat filled the air. As she began to fill their glasses with water from the sink the front door hinges squeaked loudly. Oiling them was another job to do later. Wiping her hands dry and walking out into the hall Helen's slippers moved softly over the old polished tiles.

'Paul?'

Helen reached to switch on the light and the dull yellowish glow revealed an odd almost frightened expression on his face. His eyes avoided hers sliding towards the other side of the door instead. She followed them with her own.

A tall young man stood there unmoving. There was something strangely familiar about the shape of his face. It was when he gave a tentative smile that her knees shook until Helen was afraid they wouldn't hold her up. Crazy. She mustn't be so silly. This dim light was making her imagine things.

'Helen, I need to talk to you.'

It took all her strength to remove her stare from the unknown man and look at Paul.

He took hold of her limp, unresisting hand leading her away to sit at the kitchen table. From somewhere inside her confusion Helen watched this taking place in a bizarre detached way. Paul moved the water glasses away, taking the brandy bottle from the shelf and filling two large tumblers. Did he know it was the cheap cooking kind that they never drank? The roughness of it burnt all the way down her tightened throat.

'I lied to you this morning. You knew that didn't you?' His voice didn't even sound the same as it had done over breakfast. How would she have known? Helen scrunched mentally into a knot consumed with an overwhelming desire to run away from whatever words were coming next. It wasn't going to be something she wanted to hear. She was smart enough to realize that.

'That letter was from someone I hadn't ever expected to hear from again.' Paul cautiously reached for her hands but she moved deliberately back – not prepared yet to be comforted.

'There's something I should have told you a long time ago.' Tiny pinpricks of bright red embarrassment stood out on his pale cheeks. His eyes appeared drawn to the grain in the wooden table. 'I met Sarah up at Oxford and we went out together a few times.' This couldn't simply be an old girlfriend story –

they didn't matter this much. Helen waited.

'I got her pregnant. The rest of the world might have been living in the 70s with its hippies and free love but that made no difference in our case.' There was a new bitter strain to his laugh. 'Our parents whisked us down the aisle before our feet could touch the ground.' Helen poured more brandy into her glass drinking it in one swallow with no pretence at restraint. His piercing stare probed for some reaction but she refused to succumb to the urge to howl like an animal caught in a trap. Paul's words tumbled on out.

'Two 19-year-olds stuck in a small flat with no money and both studying all hours. We never stood a chance.' A sad wistfulness filled his eyes spiralling pain deep inside Helen. 'We fought non stop for a couple of months, about everything and nothing I suppose, then Sarah gave up her degree and went back home to Manchester. Nobody here knew about the marriage. Mother talked me into believing I'd had a lucky escape. The divorce was quick and that was that.'

The harsh fluorescent light seeped his usually ruddy complexion away to grey. 'After the baby was born Sarah's mother sent the adoption papers for me to sign and that was the end of it. I never saw our son.' Regret flooded through his voice.

'Until today.'

The two simple words sliced through both their hearts. The sight of both a vivid red hand mark on his face and five distinct fingernail lines dragging down Paul's right cheek made Helen aware of what she'd unknowingly done. She'd never hit anyone before in her life. It was scary how much it was possible to feel.

'How could you not tell me? Didn't you think I had the right to know?' Then, like a stack of falling dominoes, the pieces of knowledge clicked into place. Helen's words emerged eerily calm and soft. 'Your parents knew. You all agreed to lie to me didn't you?' It wasn't a question and Paul made no denial.

He chewed at the corner of his lip, something he only did when disturbed. 'Sarah wrote now because the boy unexpectedly got in touch with her. He visited her but it didn't go too well. She knew he intended to call here next so wanted to prepare me. I was going to tell you later but he turned up at the surgery this morning. I did try to call but you were out.' The whiny edge to his voice made it almost sound like her fault.

'What's his name?'

'Simon. Simon Campbell.'

Paul continued to talk unable to stop now he'd started. 'I've had to ask him to stay tonight because he's come all the way from Scotland. What else could I do?' Helen could

21

think of plenty of alternatives. The most obvious was to have told the boy to go away and leave them alone. She didn't see it then but the problem was that if Simon had left that very minute he'd still be there in all the ways that mattered.

Helen lost her usual competence almost falling over her own feet in an awkward stumble across the room. As cold water gushed from the tap and the sink filled to the brim she plunged in, holding her face under until feeling the welcoming sensation of cooling blood. Raising her head she roughly towelled her skin until it stung. Undoing the rubber band from her hair Helen slowly ran a comb through to straighten out the tangles before tying it back again – this time with a wide blue silk ribbon she took from the drawer. With great care she meticulously adjusted the ends of the bow. In the mirror the face reflected back was as calm and ordinary as ever.

'Lunch is ready. Would you mind telling everyone while I lay an extra place?' Paul's obvious confusion made a hysterical laugh bubble up inside her hurt. What did he expect?

'Are you sure?'

What did he want to know she was sure of? Sure she didn't mind his revelation of a previous wife? Sure she was okay with him having a grown-up son when he'd always said he didn't want children? Sure that it was all right he'd lied to her for ten years?

When he got no answer Paul left her alone.

CHAPTER FOUR

*'Everybody, soon or late, sits down to a
banquet of consequences.'*
Robert Louis Stevenson

Twenty interminable minutes. That was
how long they'd been sitting so far. Helen
knew because she'd watched the hands of
the clock move slowly around that many
times.

Alice and Jack had come in and sat down as
usual. They'd politely welcomed Simon
when Paul had introduced him with absolutely no semblance of surprise. No doubt
he'd succeeded in phoning *them* earlier. Jack
couldn't meet Helen's curious eyes while
Alice's expression verged on triumphant.
   Still having the weird sensation of not
really being part of the whole situation
Helen couldn't help thinking how unbear-
ably British they were all being. A man
introduces an unknown son to his family
and their only reaction is an animated dis-
cussion about the weather and how well the
gardens are doing; of course Simon helped
that along wonderfully by chatting easily

about the new garden centre he'd recently opened. Anyone would think he was no more than an ordinary guest. She didn't get it.

There was no way she could eat, it would choke her. Poking and prodding her food around the edges of the plate Helen concentrated on breathing regularly, afraid otherwise she might stop. With Simon listening intently to Jack's advice on growing peonies it gave her the opportunity to study him unobserved.

No wonder Emily Grant had smiled that way. The resemblance was so obvious although maybe not quite as much as Helen had first thought. His height and lean body were similar but Simon's face was far more sharply defined; even before middle-aged softening Paul's bones had never been that clear. In profile he reminded Helen of a hawk at rest waiting to swoop while at the same time giving the outward impression, resting casually back in the chair, of complete ease. His pure black hair matched Paul's as a young man but it was hard to imagine the ponytail gone and replaced by a regular haircut.

Unexpectedly Simon angled his head then, just enough to meet her scrutiny. A flush of shame rose in a burning heat up her pale freckled cheeks. He held onto her stare with glittering eyes that gave the fleeting impression of a gold ring caught in the sunlight. Dropping her glance guiltily back down to the congealing macaroni on her plate Helen was only too aware of Simon's satisfied smile resting on the back of her bent head.

Helen was consumed with curiosity about Sarah. Judging by Simon she was probably attractive so in that case why had Paul chosen her for his second try at marriage? Perhaps because of her quiet mousy features not despite them as she'd always believed. No chance of memories there. She'd been told often enough as a child that her kindness and good manners were what made her special. A nasty taste rose in her throat as she pondered who Paul saw at night when the lights were out?

Alice put down her knife and fork before dabbing at her mouth with the napkin, after first giving the blue paper a disdainful look, and then delicately cleared her throat. She'd been restrained all through lunch but now her gaze fixed uncompromisingly on Simon.

'So young man, what brought you here today after all these years?'

No one else would have dared to ask but Alice merely crossed her hands neatly in her lap and waited. Simon didn't hurry, first taking a long slow drink of water, and then managing a slight taut smile before finally replying. With the hard found words his previously soft Scottish accent became

26

more noticeable.

'Well it's a long story Mrs. Barton and I know Paul has to get back to work so maybe it's better kept until tonight?' His controlled assurance made it plain Simon didn't much care if Alice minded or not. The answer was his to tell when he was ready.

'No Simon it won't keep. I think we deserve an answer now. By the way is it usual in your part of the country to call parents by their first names?' Their words bounced backwards and forwards like a game of table tennis played with lethal weapons.

The shallowly disguised animosity, which had been there all the time, rose to the surface of Simon's hardening glance. It made Helen's throat constrict with fear and silently she willed Paul to do something but he remained motionless as if frozen in stone.

'I'm sorry if I offended you.' That apology was a lie if ever Helen had heard one. 'If you want to hear the whole thing now then of course you shall. And by the way even in the wilds of Scotland we retain some manners but as I don't consider Paul to be my father I don't feel I have to apply the usual rules. Do please feel free to correct me if I'm wrong but I think it's probably accurate to say that in the nearly thirty years I've been alive he's barely given me a thought from one year to the next. He's done absolutely *nothing* to deserve the name father from

27

me.' Helen jumped in her seat as the word nothing snapped out like a broken rubber band. Simon's unreadable expression slid across again like a mask.

Alice's rage swamped the room; no one ever dared to speak to her like that. The rigidly held jaw, throbbing blue vein on her forehead and sharp fingernails digging into her hands were clearly at odds with the placatory smile she fixed on. Her reply, when she calmed enough to make one, was as plainly false as Simon's supposed apology.

'I should have been more considerate, do forgive me.'

Simon barely nodded an acknowledgement.

'Mother I think that's enough.' Finally Paul intervened and Helen felt herself exhaling a deep relief. 'Simon, would you join me in my study for a few minutes?'

Helen needed to move, if she sat there any longer she'd be sick. Her stomach was already churning with the tension. She hated upsets. Making coffee should have been a peaceful option but her kitchen's comforting familiarity had been leeched away by nastiness. A steady rain lashed at the windows beating her poor daffodils down to the ground. Only for them could Helen feel any sympathy.

The kettle boiled and she filled the cups, relishing the warm steam against her chilled skin. As she placed one in front of Jack she tried to dredge up some sliver of compassion for the worn out man dabbing with a handkerchief at his eyes but was stopped by the remembrance of his dishonesty. Pouring out two more coffees she walked towards the study – ten years was long enough to be kept out.

The only sound breaking the weighty silence came from Simon's fingers idly tapping on the worn arms of the old red leather chair. Standing at the window Paul stared blankly out into the grey early afternoon sky misery plainly carved into every line of his body.

'Cream and sugar Simon?' His only response was a curt shake of the head. As she passed the cup to him her fingertips briefly touched his unexpectedly warm skin. Paul attempted to take his coffee from her but was let down by trembling hands that spilt the hot liquid over the papers spread on the desk. Grabbing a handful of tissues he half-heartedly mopped at the mess before abandoning the sodden lump and slumping heavily down into the other chair.

With his head cradled by cupped hands Paul's loud wrenching sobs filled the room. Helen was transfixed, outside of television or the cinema she'd never seen a man cry before. Her immediate reaction was to reach out her hand in comfort but with the evidence of Paul's betrayal sitting so calmly in the other chair she recoiled. Simon's shrewd cat-like eyes watched Paul with impassive curiosity – what was he thinking? She couldn't begin to imagine nor was she sure of wanting to. It should have been obvious after all these years what would happen next.

The telephone rang six times before Helen reluctantly gave in and answered it, plainly no one else would. From somewhere she found her polite doctor's wife voice and was able to carry on a conversation. When she hung up neither man spoke.

'Paul that was James. He's wondering where you are because Mrs. Penlee called to complain that you're late visiting her. I told him you hadn't felt too well after lunch but that you'd be on your way soon. I didn't know what else to say.' The message from his partner didn't appear to register. 'I'll show Simon to his room so you can get back to work.' Helen was willing Paul to leave so she wouldn't have to go on seeing his hurt.

Slowly unfurling his long legs and standing up Simon gave her a sly almost teasing glance. That unsettled Helen enough without him then swiftly picking up the tray and leading the way out into the hall.

Forced to choose between following him and being left alone with Paul, Helen went.

CHAPTER FIVE

*'Give me one friend, just one, who meets the
needs of all my varying moods.'*
Esther M. Clarke

Simon casually threw a red checked tea towel
in her direction. Helen ignored the wet cup
held in his outstretched hand picking one up
from the drainer instead. She dried it very
methodically before putting it back in the
cupboard. He stopped, soapsuds dripping
unnoticed down his tanned forearm, and
stared intently through the streams of rain
running down the window.

'The garden looks good Helen. Is that your
doing or Paul's?' Keeping her hands busy by
continuing to wipe the dishes an impulsively
honest answer popped out. 'Alice had neatly
regimented rows of matching flowers so after
we moved in I ripped them all out and planted vegetables instead.' Simon's spontaneous
warm laugh filled the room and without
conscious intent Helen joined in. Guiltily she
threw the wet towel down on the counter.

Simon was the enemy, he'd destroyed her
peace of mind, it didn't matter that it wasn't
his fault in the first place. Blaming him was

the safer path.

'I'll show you to your room if you're ready.' Helen made herself ignore the way his lips twitched humorously at her sudden change of behaviour. All the way up the spiral staircase she chattered inanely on about the history of the house as if he cared a fig about the old vicars who'd lived there. She knew it was wrong to be wondering how huge her bottom must look from behind in these too tight jeans.

At least the guest room was decent since she'd repapered it a couple of months ago in bold yellow and white striped paper; thank goodness Alice wasn't able to get upstairs to see what Helen had done to the room her precious baby had been born in. After rattling off the vagaries of the central heating system and showing him the nearby bathroom she left giving Simon no further chance for conversation.

Leaning forward, her hands resting on the table for support, Helen gasped in vain for air as if she'd run a couple of miles. She tried a few deep-calming breaths but that didn't work. One glance in the mirror confirmed that her cheeks really were a hot flaming pink. Helen flung open the door and stepped outside gratefully allowing the heavy drizzle to soothe the burning angry heat inside her. Dragging the ribbon loose she shook her hair out, not bothered if it turned from straight to frizz. Later on it might matter when she couldn't do anything with it for dinner but right now Helen only revelled in the cooling effect of the soft rain.

'Trying to imitate a water baby Helen dear?'

Julie's disjointed voice floated through the thick curtain of rain.

'Roger said you'd called earlier so I came over for a cup of tea but perhaps we could have it indoors seeing as it didn't occur to me to put my swimsuit on to visit.' A fragile smile tinged Helen's eyes. As they linked arms and walked indoors Helen kept up her end of an ordinary conversation, all the time going crazy planning how to explain what had happened. It was going to sound utterly ridiculous no matter how she told the story.

Julie's deep brown eyes followed Helen around the kitchen as she busied herself for as long as possible – filling up the kettle and turning it on before taking a towel to her hair and rubbing vigorously. An effort to pull a comb through failed as it broke in half in the impossible tangle of wet curls.

'So what's the big sigh for? Am I that unwelcome?'

Helen could only shake her head, gaining a few more minutes by making the tea and shuffling some biscuits around on a plate. With everything on the table there was no choice but to sit. As she picked up the tea-pot to pour Julie stopped her with a gentle touch on her arm.

'What ever is it Helen? What's wrong?'

Those few words were all it took to break open the days bottled up control. Tears cascaded down Helen's cheeks, flowing as if they might never stop. Slowing them to a quiet sniffle she blew hard on a crumpled tissue salvaged from her pocket.

'I don't know where to begin Julie, I just don't.'

'Copy my namesake – pretend you're singing that idiotic song from 'The Sound of Music' and start at the very beginning.' Julie's ordinary bright laughter jarred.

'You aren't going to believe this...'

'For heavens sake get on with it you daft thing.'

'Paul got a letter in the post this morning.'

'Well that's really exciting news. Presumably it wasn't an ordinary bill or a letter from a grateful patient so put me out of my misery please.' Before Helen could decide how, Julie carried on. 'No hang on, let me guess first. I bet it was from an old girlfriend revealing a love child Paul never knew he had and demanding money for her silence. Am I close?' Julie giggled but Helen couldn't join in, her hands twisting in knots as she struggled to explain the unexplainable. Through her shame she saw some brief understanding dawn on Julie's face.

'Hey this is your Paul we're talking about? You know serious, steady, responsible Paul.'

Helen's took a desperately needed breath before her answer emerged, her voice small and brittle. 'Unfortunately you're closer to the truth than you could possibly imagine. Paul and his parents decided that the fact he'd been married before to a girl called Sarah was one little detail I didn't need to know about before our wedding. The second little detail is a twenty-nine year old son called Simon who's upstairs in the guest bedroom.'

Pushing the chair away Helen walked over by the window where the soaked garden lay as dark and wrung out as her heart. The only way she could continue was by turning away from Julie's horrified face. 'The marriage broke up after a few months and the baby was adopted without Paul ever seeing him. Sarah wrote to warn him that the boy had already visited her and was planning to come here next. So guess who turned up at the surgery this morning wanting to play Happy Families?'

'This is crazy, Helen.'

'Tell me about it. I know it is but that six foot tall young man proves it, you'll know when you see him trust me.'

'Does he look like Paul?' That wasn't an easy question to answer.

'Well yes and no. There's no doubt whose son he is.' She nearly choked on the word 'son'. 'His face is similar and his hair is exactly like Paul's used to be but his eyes are very different – an odd sort of golden colour.'

'Intriguing.'

The sudden opening of the kitchen door shut them up like two naughty schoolgirls caught smoking in the toilets.

'Oh I'm sorry Helen, I didn't know you had a visitor.'

Apologize and go back upstairs – that was all she wanted him to do, it wasn't too much to ask surely? But of course he couldn't do that. Simon lounged against the wall in his irritating calm way plainly waiting for an introduction. All Helen managed was to state his name – no way could she call him her stepson even though she supposed in a way he was – it would have gagged her.

There it was again, the charming smile and friendly innocence he'd practiced on them all earlier. Within a few minutes he and Julie were chatting away like old friends. Helen had almost forgotten how attractive boys used to find Julie before her controlling husband had squashed her exuberance like a dead fly. Helen's simmering hurt only allowed her to see her friend as a traitor.

'Would you like a cup of tea Simon?' He could barely hold back from laughing aloud at her clumsy interruption. Accepting the cup she poured he thanked her with exaggerated politeness before excusing himself and disappearing back upstairs.

In the uneasy silence he left behind neither woman spoke immediately. The two had never seriously quarrelled before but Julie's next words brought them close. 'God, he's gorgeous Helen, and not much younger than us either.' Helen couldn't believe what she was hearing. Her eyes must have said what her voice couldn't because Julie's soft eyes darkened and her smile faded. Helen wanted nothing more than for her to leave.

'I need to get on and fix dinner.' It was only four o'clock. Julie treated her statement as if it were true, although they both knew otherwise.

'That's okay, the children will be home soon and I need to pop into the shop for a few things first. I'll talk to you tomorrow. Take care of yourself, okay.' Julie moved sympathetically towards her but the offered kindness was too late and Helen stepped back away from reach. For the first time in years they parted without hugging.

Helen was left desolate and empty; on no other day had she ever longed for her parents quite so badly. It was all right for her sister Lucy having them next door but thousands of miles away in Australia wasn't where

Helen wanted them right now.

It was lucky she couldn't hear the conversation in the next room – it would have sunk her spirits even lower.

CHAPTER SIX

'For of all sad words of tongue or pen, the saddest are these, "It might have been."'
John Greenleaf Whittier

'Did you see that stupid creature acting as though she knew all about Sarah and the boy?'

A satisfied look spread unpleasantly across Alice's face but the agitation set off one of her coughing fits, as her hands flailed at Jack she struggled to catch her breath. Her irritation was palpable as he slowly limped over with some water. The glass was snatched from his hand with no thanks.

'Our grandson has certainly grown into a handsome young man. We may have made a mistake letting him go in the first place.' That was a rare admission. 'Of course his mother was a cheap little tart so we couldn't have known how the boy would turn out.' Jack made no comment. 'If Helen tries to keep Paul away from Simon she'll have me to deal with. I'll soon remind her whose names are on the deed to this house. I only hope I live long enough to see Paul get rid of her.'

39

Jack's cheeks flushed, the thin veins spreading in a purple maze over his thin skin. 'It's not very nice of you to talk about Helen like that, dear. She does so much for us and she's a good wife to Paul. I always thought he was wrong not to tell her everything before they married.'

Alice rolled her chair around to ensure he could see the contempt on her face more clearly. 'Oh shut up you silly old fool. Why my father ever thought you had any sense is beyond me. Can't you see what a good position this puts us in? They'd better watch out or we might decide to change our wills. I'm sure Simon would be only too appreciative.' The words were bitterly spat from her snarling mouth.

With every day it became more impossible for Jack to remember the girl he'd fallen so in love with nearly sixty years ago.

It had been just another Saturday night dance in the local church hall – a way for them all to escape for a few hours. Only a glimmer of light had peeked through the dense blackout as he walked up the path with Johnny, his pilot, and Tony, the rear gunner, the others joking about what they'd do with the women they were sure to hook up with. Jack remembered running his fingers around the back of his neck where the rough uniform itched and smelled damp after the two-mile walk from camp. When the door opened the warmth and sound of the band had drifted out. They'd finished their cigarettes and stubbed them out in the gravel.

They always checked the dance floor first for new girls and he'd seen her straight away, naturally already dancing with one of the Yanks, her bright yellow dress shimmering like a ray of sunlight. Amazingly she'd caught his eye and smiled a challenge to him. He was usually the shy one but for once his mates hadn't had to encourage him.

The red-faced Sergeant from Pittsburgh blustered a bit but reluctantly gave her up. Jack could see himself now waltzing them over by the buffet table because it was quieter, the meagre spread of unwanted potted meat sandwiches and weak lemonade meant there wasn't exactly a crowd around.

Alice had told him her name then with a bewitching smile reaching from deep beyond her soft blue eyes all the way to her dainty white shoed feet. There had been no protest either when he'd dared to slip an arm around her tiny waist. It had been close enough for Jack to smell the delicate lavender perfume in her long black hair caught up with a yellow silk ribbon to match her dress.

By Sunday afternoon he was sitting on a hard backed chair in her parents' front room, drinking tea and eating dry scones with the rationed scrape of margarine. Enid and William Bosworthy could have given lessons to the intelligence services as expert as they were at grilling young men about their prospects. As a navigator who'd already miraculously survived ten missions over Germany, Jack's weren't exactly promising. It was somehow winkled out of him that he'd completed a couple of years of law studies before joining up, and that he wouldn't be averse to clerking in Mr. Bosworthy's law office if by some miracle he survived.

During it all Alice sat demurely in the corner, her delicate hands smoothing down the pretty blue silk dress, only occasionally meeting his eyes and blushing delicately when she did so, like any well brought up young woman. It had only added to her charm.

When his leave was up the following week Jack found he was an engaged man with the promise of a job and help buying a house if he could stay alive. A crash landing in Belgium helped him to manage his part of the bargain leaving him with a dodgy leg and life long guilt for surviving. The nightmares came less often these days but when they did Johnny and Tony's faces were as clear as ever. They'd never aged or been disappointed. Sometimes he wondered who'd been lucky.

He held onto the memory of those first five

years; they were his consolation when things were bad. Alice had been the perfect wife – beautiful, loving and kind. But when the expected babies didn't arrive it had started. The time spent in bed together went from magically special to being, in Alice's eyes, for one purpose only. By the time they were 'successful' something irretrievable had been lost.

It had begun with mild sarcasm when he was five minutes later coming home than promised, and crept insidiously through their life, culminating in Alice turning away in bed when he reached for her and not even bothering to hide her distaste. His desperate efforts to please plainly struck her as mere weakness.

The fact that she made a group of similarly unsatisfied friends didn't help, particularly that nasty Emily Grant at the shop. Alice had worn him down with her constant nagging for a better house – God knows the old rectory with its huge mortgage had frightened him more than the Germans ever did. All the time there was a constant record kept of what they had or rather didn't have compared to everyone else. Jack's banishment to the spare bedroom by the time Paul started school, ostensibly so Alice could get her correct amount of beauty sleep, came by then as nothing short of a relief.

Because of Jack's silence poor Paul was groomed within an inch of his life, steered firmly away from playing with 'inferior' village boys, and sent away to a boarding school they could barely afford at only eight. It added another rung to Jack's ladder of guilt to know he'd made no effort to interfere; only too glad that Alice's obsession with Paul and his future took the heat off him. Medicine was decided upon as the most suitable profession so Paul had become a doctor. Jack had always been too afraid to ask whether or not his son was happy.

Jack wished he had the guts to go and tell Helen how sorry he was but the war had taken the bravery out of him. He'd come to the conclusion that people have an allotment of courage for their lifetime and his was used up by those years. After all the pain and loss, for the rest of his life all he wanted was peace at whatever cost.

Helen slumped over the table as though the blood had stopped flowing through her veins. Wearily she went to the back door, kicked off the hated slippers, and pushed her feet into the old gardening shoes she always left there. Ignoring the thick squelchy mud she walked in between the rows of carrots, pulling enough out of the damp loose soil to cook with dinner. Helen shook off the worst of the dirt before bringing them towards her nose to smell the fresh earthy richness clinging to them.

'Nothing quite like it is there?'

Simon stood right behind her on the path – grinning confidently, his hair loose and hanging almost to his shoulders. It seemed to have a life of its own moving lightly in the breeze.

'What the hell are you doing creeping around?' He took a step back raising his hands in a gesture of surrender. 'Hey I'm sorry; I didn't mean to startle you. Fresh air seemed tempting that's all.'

A frequently uttered admonition of her mothers echoed in Helen's mind – treat people, as you'd like to be treated and if you can't say something nice keep quiet. A good scream and cry was really what she needed but too many years of ingrained reservations overcame that. On went the apologetic smile and out came the kind, if untruthful, words.

'No, I'm the one who should be sorry.'

'Maybe you should but don't pretend to be if you really aren't. I've had more than enough of that today.' His bitterness was sharp enough to cut with a knife. 'I should have left well alone, my parents tried to warn me but I wouldn't listen – typical hardheaded stubborn male I suppose.' With a resigned shrug of his shoulders some of Simon's pain needled its way into her. Helen couldn't begin to imagine what it must be like to know that your parents weren't truly yours, after all there were generations of Trewarrens in the village cemetery – she knew where she was from.

'Are the parents you grew up with good people Simon?' Straightforward love spread across his usually unrevealing face. 'They're the best, I was lucky. They took me in when I was only a few weeks old and I grew up in their lovely old house. When I was five they had their own baby so I have a sister, Aileen. They never treated me any differently to her though.'

Helen held her breath tightly wanting to hear about Sarah but not daring to ask.

'I grew up knowing that I'd been chosen specially to be part of the family and wasn't remotely curious until a girlfriend found that strange.' The struggle to bury his anger played out across his skin. 'It's too easy to track down adoption details these days. They don't ask enough questions about why you're doing it and before you know there it is in black and white.'

Simon's kicked at the earth with the toe of his muddy shoe. 'It's about as hard as it gets to come face to face with someone whose life you've essentially ruined merely by being born.' Helen was held by the full force of his previously golden eyes, now dark as treacle, there was nowhere else to look. 'She's had such a hard time of it Helen, never went back to college, stuck in a dead-end job and still living with parents who've never ceased to express their shame in her for thirty years.' His unspoken comparison with Paul's apparently charmed life resonated uncomfortably.

In the fading afternoon light the nearby streetlight turned on casting a yellow glow over that end of the garden. 'I must go and start dinner – we usually eat about seven if that's okay with you?'

Simon reached out lightly touching her shoulder, 'You don't have to try so hard you know none of this is your fault.' His frank sympathy made Helen want to cry until there were no tears left but the remembrance of who he was returned and she turned away.

One corner of Alice's white lace curtains fell slyly back into place as Helen's solitary footsteps crunched down the gravel path, almost running back to the lighted kitchen and the illusion of safety.

CHAPTER SEVEN

*'If we resist our passions, it is more through
their weakness than from our strength.'*
Francois De La Rochefoucaud

Through the early evening gloom the slump
of Simon's darkening form at the top of the
garden was too clear. Very deliberately Helen
allowed the blind to fall down and snapped
back into ordinary household competence. It
soothed her to scrub, peel and chop until
before long dinner was in the oven cooking.
Soon the room would fill with the comforting
aroma of roasting meat, and then it would be
normal again, an everyday dinner like hundreds of others she'd prepared over the years.
There were more greasy marks on her jeans
where she'd absentmindedly wiped her
hands yet again. It was time to go and tidy up
if she didn't want to elicit more Alice comments.

Stepping warm and pink from the shower
Helen vigorously rubbed the towel over her
rather dry neglected skin, grabbed the tub
of lotion off the shelf and quickly massaged
some into her arms and legs. It was the

cheap stuff bought from Livvy at the school Christmas Fair and smelt oddly of sour apples. The worn and grey look of the clean underwear she pulled from the drawer made Helen grimace. Her next load of washing had better include bleach.

Unusually Helen stood still then in front of the mirror. The reflection showed a body more generously curved than in the past, she tried to phrase it that nicer way in her mind, but still in fairly good shape. Not very exciing maybe but not repulsive either. It could be worse. As her fingers checked to see if she had a double chin yet, thankfully everything was holding firm in that direction, she noticed Paul perched on the corner of the bed, his face taut and serious. Taking off his tie he dropped it down on the quilt and she got the clear sense of no energy being left in him.

The good loving side of Helen yearned to hug him and say they'd be all right but it was too soon. Truthfully it wasn't anger now more of a deep sorrow, a disappointment. For a glance their eyes met before both looked away. From the wardrobe she chose a plain dark blue dress and put it on. The zip stuck slightly at the small of her back but she wriggled until it did up rather than ask for help.

'Sherry?' Strangely enough she waited for Paul to make his usual joke about their surreptitiously hidden bottle. It didn't happen. Her reply sounded level and calm – nothing but ordinary sounding Helen. 'Yes please.' They sipped the pale liquid silently wrapped in misunderstanding.

The two things Helen had always admired most in Paul – his honesty and humour – were missing tonight. If she asked him a question, and a thousand swirled inside her head, how could she know any more if the answer were the truth? And as for jokes and fun, something they'd always happily shared, well they were a million miles from that.

At least putting on her make-up would avoid the need to speak for a few minutes, of course applying mascara with slightly trembling hands without poking her eye out might be a challenge. It didn't help that Paul's watchful reflection filled the mirror.

'Helen.' His eyes pleaded as much as his rough edged voice. Later, when things were worse, she would wonder what might have happened if she'd made a different choice? Her answer was to take a quick glance at her watch and then go over to close the curtains on the darkening evening. 'I can't stop now. If I don't see to the lamb it'll be cremated.' He didn't persevere and she walked away.

Twelve measured chimes rang out from the church clock, its regularity so comforting. It always had the power to make her feel less alone especially in the middle of a long night. Listening to Paul's steady rhythmic breathing on the pillow next to her it bewildered Helen how he could sleep after the day they'd had. If she lay there any longer she'd scream out loud.

Quietly slipping out from under the covers she went to sit in the bay window, pulling the curtain back a few inches to look onto the deserted street, and releasing the latch allowing the cool fresh air to stroke her face. The evening replayed over and over but the only disquiet she found there seemed to be within her.

It had been so startlingly ordinary with perfectly cooked food and amiable conversation. Simon was planning to leave in the morning but the relief she should have felt didn't come. It had all been disconcertingly simple. They'd had a strong marriage before this so they could again. Other people survived worse.

Paul's body under the covers was genuinely still – it wasn't hard to tell if he was faking sleep. Tiptoeing across the carpet Helen lifted her ancient pink dressing gown down from the peg to put it on, tying the belt firmly. She had doubts that warm milk worked for insomnia when you knew why you couldn't sleep but there was nothing to lose by trying.

'Couldn't you sleep either?'

She slapped a hand across her mouth to stop from screaming. The small light over the counter cast a ghostly glow over the canisters and mugs spreading to include in its range Simon, in an old grey T-shirt, sweatpants and bare feet, comfortably sprawled in her own favourite rocking chair.

'What the hell are you doing down here in the middle of the night?'

'I could ask you the same?' he grinned and laughed softly.

'You have no right to ask me anything. It's my house. I can do what I like.' Helen cringed at her childish words. 'Sorry. I'm not normally touchy like this – honestly.'

His warm sure fingers touched her arm, 'Sit down Helen, and let me pour you a cup of tea for a change.' She had no idea why she did as he'd asked.

'It's my turn to apologize and this time you'll let me. I made a big mistake raking all this business up. I was perfectly content and now I've made a real mess of everything.' Facing him across the table, Helen put both hands around the steaming mug he'd placed nearby. His contrition pulled her unwillingly in so that when his next question came guilt made her answer honestly.

'I assume Paul never talked much about his time at university?'

It was hard to push the words out of her reluctant throat. 'We both grew up here but he's ... quite a bit older than me and our families didn't mix socially so I only really got to know him when he returned to practice here. I lived at home still and my social life was pretty limited.' Simon's quiet listening encouraged her to carry on all the while wishing it didn't make her sound so desperate.

'He was single, good looking, and intelligent. I was inexperienced and flattered he'd even look twice at me so I was relieved he didn't want to swap past love stories because I honestly didn't have any.'

Simon's leaned across, glaring furiously at her. 'Oh don't talk rubbish, you're an attractive woman, he can't have been your first serious boyfriend?' Helen didn't understand why he sounded angry, angry for her. 'Why do you keep putting yourself down? You've already got Alice doing it for you while dear old Jack keeps silent. I'm sure Paul loves you but he doesn't exactly stand up for you too much either does he?'

'How dare you? You know nothing about my marriage or me and that's the way I'd like to keep it. For God's sake go back to Scotland and stay there. The only thing we'll ever agree on is that you should never have come in the first place.'

Scraping the chair legs viciously on the

tiles Helen stumbled towards the door, hardly able to see through her tears. Simon blocked the way as her hand reached for the doorknob and before she could draw another breath his mouth came down on hers crushing her fury. One arm wrapped around her tightly while with the other his calloused fingers stroked their way through her hair. There was a dim sense of a hand loosening her belt, sliding inside and upwards until he lighted on her bare skin setting every nerve on fire. Reality returned and with its harsh awareness her traitorous body was finally able to pull away.

As Helen ran from the room in panic the thin chink of light under Alice's door and the click of the latch went unnoticed.

It was all she could do to make it upstairs to their bathroom before retching uncontrollably, clinging to the cold basin in utter disgust. None of her crashing movements made any impact on Paul's relaxed snores. The hollow emptiness in her stomach brought some measure of control to Helen's disturbed mind.

They'd had a difficult day, been emotionally upset and overreacted – that was all. No one else knew so no real harm had been done. Helen tried to close the door on her memory of how it'd felt. She hadn't had a clue before that kiss because it had never been like that with Paul. Mutual attraction and pleasant sex between two slightly lonely people had given them a good marriage and it would keep on doing so. She would make sure of that.

Pulling back the covers Helen slid under, wrapping her chilled body around Paul's back. It wasn't difficult to wriggle around, 'accidentally' poke her foot into his calf, anything to wake him up. His bleary eyes barely focused as he turned around but she couldn't easily meet their questioning shine. Helen's only answer was to quickly remove her nightdress, before she could have second thoughts, and press her body along his length. He didn't need any more encouragement, now she could let him take over and blot out her shame.

Afterwards he gave her the usual warm cuddle before drifting back to sleep. Considering she almost never initiated sex and after all that had happened he was plainly only too grateful to ask why? Helen bottled up the unshed tears lying corpse-like until the clock struck three and exhaustion finally claimed her.

'Is it morning?' The sunlight gushing in through the open curtains hurt her burning eyes. Paul's face radiated relief for some reason that Helen couldn't fathom. She searched through the painful fog for an explanation but none came. 'No darling, it's four in the afternoon. I was beginning to think you'd never wake up.' The laugh he gave sounded forced and awkward. 'I suppose you were worn out after yesterday, no wonder really.' Unfortunately then the memories became only too clear. She wished they hadn't. Paul's worry irritated like rough sandpaper and it was hard to stand it.

'I'm going to have a shower.' She had the awful urge to smack his hand away as he helped her into the bathroom, ran the water to exactly the right temperature, found a fresh towel and clean underwear. 'It's okay Paul. I'm fine.' It must have been convincing as first his face relaxed and then he placed a gentle kiss on her forehead. It was safer to let him think he was right.

CHAPTER EIGHT

*'Never rely on the glory of the morning or the
smiles of your mother-in-law.'*
Japanese proverb

'So have you heard from the errant stepson
recently?'

Helen sipped her tea, watching soft rain
fall on the potted pink and white tulips
flourishing outside Julie's back door, before
answering. For once it was she who was
tense and her friend relaxed; Roger's business trip to Exeter for a couple of days had
removed the anxious hunch from Julie's
shoulders. Livvy and John's carefree voices
drifted down from upstairs – there was no
need to be quiet.

'We had a standard thank you letter, that's
all.' A lump of unhappiness rested in Helen's
heart but the words that could have freed it
were too firmly stuck. An uncomfortable
quiet descended.

'I'd better go or I'll be late for Alice's
Mothers' Union meeting.' Unusually Julie
didn't joke about Helen's resemblance to a
doormat so instead she made her own feeble
effort, 'you know that would get me in

trouble.' The warm hug Julie gave her almost broke through the stupid reserve punishing them both. It hinted at so much. Saying, please talk, share what's really bothering you. And then maybe it also said, push me a little more and I'll tell you what's burning me up inside. Neither woman had enough courage for that first move.

Helen dawdled her way home. With her hand resting on the doorknob it was all she could do to make herself go in. Alice's voice rang out before she had the chance for a strengthening breath. 'Helen dear, could you bring my green coat in please?' The pleasant way of being asked combined with the friendly smile Helen received entering the room wasn't normal. 'I wouldn't ask but Jack's dropped off to sleep so I didn't want to wake him.' Since when had that bothered her?

Well she could make an effort one more time in return. 'I'll drive the car around and then come in for you.' Another smile, no admonition about hurrying up, no sniffy comments about Helen's jeans and T-shirt.

Negotiating the path into the church hall from the road meant an excruciatingly slow passage on the uneven gravel with walking sticks. Always there were complaints – either Helen was holding her arm wrong or walking too fast or too slow but this morning brought none of that. Inside, Helen settled Alice into a seat at the front so she wouldn't miss anything. She wanted to get away before the appreciative bubble burst.

How could she not have known? All the signs were there for anyone with half a brain to recognize. The straightening of Alice's shoulders, one twisted hand fingering the tightly permed hair to make sure it was perfectly in place.

Violet Barnett's imposing figure arrived beside them. Helen had watched her making her way up through the room – condescending to throw a few well-chosen words here and there in the direction of those who merited the attentions of the vicar's wife. 'Good morning Alice, how are you today dear?'

Helen took a covert glance at the woman who always had the power to make her (and surely others too) feel incredibly guilty over sins not even committed. As it was only early spring her firmly corseted figure remained encased in a sensible dark tweed suit; the starched white blouse underneath her single concession to the season.

'I'm very well thank you, Violet.' As one of the few permitted this familiarity Alice relished in the privilege. 'I have to tell you about the lovely phone call I got from my grandson this morning.' Every atom of Helen's strength was needed to return the smile while hoping the colour draining away from her face didn't look as obvious as it felt from her side. 'He's coming for my birthday next week. Said he absolutely had to seeing as I'm going to be 80, isn't that kind of him? He really is a dear boy.' Her expression was an encyclopedia of triumph.

'That's wonderful.' Mrs. Barnett fixed her clear hazel-eyed gaze on Helen. 'You're such an inspiring example of practical Christianity to the rest of us the way you've all welcomed him into the family.' The two older women wore matching self-righteous expressions, probably expecting to hear appropriate words of forgiveness in support of Paul. As if they'd be so generous if their own husbands revealed something similar. Why on earth was she supposed to be so damn noble? The choking sensation in her throat threatened to clamp down on the lies Helen attempted to force out.

'Well we've done the best we can and he's a very pleasant young man, it would be hard not to like him.'

A glance at her watch steadied Helen. 'I must be going now Alice, I'll be back at 12.'

'There's no need for that, I'll gladly bring Alice home.' Violet Barnett's face had what Helen and Julie often referred to as her 'Holier than thou and everyone else' look. 'Of course you know you're always welcome to stay and join us? We're discussing the story of the Prodigal Son today and your insights would be most welcome.' Helen studied the floor closely not trusting herself to speak. She managed to demur politely, let them enjoy talking about her later – they would anyway.

Helen's shaky fingers automatically dialled the surgery number – housework could wait. First she had to go through the usual performance with Paul's receptionist Josie. The good doctor's wife side of her had to remember to ask after Josie's daughter now recovering from chickenpox or the word would go around that Helen was aloof and uncaring. That really wasn't fair as she did care but sometimes the scrutiny was all too much.

She had to find out if Paul knew about Simon coming although in her mind there was really no doubt. His dear mother was bound to have taken great pleasure in calling him straight away. What needled the most was that it simply wouldn't have occurred to him to turn around then and phone her, he didn't mean to be hurtful, and she knew that but that didn't make her feel any better. Maybe she should hang up before being put through, Paul wouldn't understand her upset reasoning, the borderline childishness at being left out like an outcast from the popular group at school.

He didn't care for her bothering him at work unless it was an emergency and this definitely wouldn't count as one in his mind. The tired and fed up Monday morning sound was in his voice but Helen carried on anyway. 'Did you know Simon is coming next week?' His sigh told her more than a whole string of sentences. 'Yes dear. I'll talk to you about it over lunch. See you later.'

Helen slammed the phone down although the only person that satisfied was herself because he'd already hung up. She could hardly call Julie for reassurance seeing as her friend wouldn't know why any was needed.

Whatever had possessed her to have her hair done like this? It had looked good on the girl in the magazine and her hairdresser had been so convincing. Instead of a confidence boost she felt like a freak. Forty pounds worth of highlights and drastic styling were scrubbed away in the shower – the hair washed until her scalp tingled and then left to dry into something vaguely close to her own natural curls again.

Throwing on an old white T-shirt and dirty jeans Helen furiously hoed the cab-bage bed. The hotter the sun warmed her skin the more satisfied she became as sweat and dirt trickled down her neck and back. As footsteps crunched on the path she kept her head bent. 'Fix the tea yourself Paul, I'm busy.' It was tiring making things easy for him all the time. He could make the effort for a change.

'Don't worry about that, we'll manage ourselves, I only came to say hello.'

Leaning back on her heels and staring into Simon's smiling face Helen was totally unaware of radiating a welcome flushed with the sun, her face bare and unadorned. She wouldn't have believed how that one casual look encouraged Simon's intentions – the ones that weren't good to start with. It did something deeper too but that would take much longer for either to realize.

If she didn't go in, tidy up and join them far too much would be read into her absence. Walking back to the house with Simon and making ordinary conversation some of the tenseness left her. By the time dinner was over she'd come to the pleasant conclusion that whatever it was that had so unbalanced her no longer threatened. She couldn't imagine how it ever had done.

At last Helen could leave them all drinking coffee and start on the dishes in peace. Her hands swirled idly around the hot soapy water having already washed the same plate three times. The unexpected shock of firm hands grasping her waist made her jump. 'Sim...'

Her mouth clamped shut. Paul was standing there next to her, confusion filling his face. She watched him decide not to ask why she'd thought it was Simon. There was an air of carefulness between them now that was disconcerting. All their previous openness and trust was measured out in tiny doses these days.

'I thought I'd give you a hand so we can get to bed earlier.' His hand moved to rub her back but the effect of his body touching hers made Helen want to pull away. 'I'm tired Paul, grab a tea towel if you want to help.'

Polishing the taps was always the last thing she did before finishing, just like her mother, and the stainless steel reflected Paul's sad face. This was her marriage, her life. She had to do better than this. A cautious kiss on his pale cheek was all it took. His deep blue eyes flooded with love as he pulled her towards him. There it came again the good, safe feeling she so relied on. This wasn't worth risking for anything. Like sneaky teenagers they kissed backed up against the kitchen counter.

Alice's petulant voice calling out penetrated their fun. 'Helen, bring me a glass of water.' The woman had appalling timing but Helen didn't find it hard to drag up the grace to be benevolent. Laughingly she sent Paul on to warm the bed – he didn't argue – murmuring in her ear before he left precisely what he was looking forward to so much. At the sink Helen even let the tap run a full minute, making sure the water was good and cold the way Alice liked it.

The wheelchair was stationed by the window; closing time at the pub with the opportunity for tucking away vindictive memories of those who couldn't walk quite straight wasn't something willingly missed. Swiveling herself around Alice's piercing eyes, lit from behind by the small green-fringed lamp, effectively pinned Helen to the carpet.

'You can put the glass down. I don't want it.'

Helen's heart raced uncomfortably and her throat was dry and gritty.

'Listen well to what I'm saying. I know exactly what's going on between you and Simon. I heard you in the kitchen the last time he was here and then I saw the pair of you in the garden this afternoon. My body might be in a wheelchair but my mind isn't. You won't make a fool of my son. If I see just one more thing I'll tell Paul and don't think I won't.'

Helen had no problem believing. There was no point defending herself. Alice wouldn't tolerate excuses.

'Get out of my sight and you'd better remember every word I've said.'

Helen remembered while Paul gazed into her eyes, his hands removing the sheer black nightdress from her, almost tearing it in his eagerness. She remembered when he collapsed satisfied on top of her. She would have to remember every single minute Simon was here. The church clock struck the hours away. While she remembered.

CHAPTER NINE

'Silence is a text easy to misread.'
A.A. Attanasio 'The Eagle and the Sword'

This was all right. She could do this.

Sipping a glass of homemade lemonade Helen flipped happily through the pile of fabric swatches on her lap. The soft peach was pretty but maybe a little too feminine? Paul had expressed a preference for the dark green but she found it too dark. Maybe a Swedish style blue and white would work?

She was proud of having managed the Simon problem so well. Making sure not to be alone with him again. Appearing very obvious in her affection for Paul, which hadn't been difficult. All this rubbish about people not being responsible for their behaviour where love was concerned was nothing but an excuse. She'd proved all you needed was self-discipline. Paul should be easy enough to convince that the time was right now for them to start their own family. She'd be taking slight advantage of his desire to please her these days but hopefully that wasn't too wrong.

The doorbell upset her comfortable reverie. Someone was shouting which meant she'd better go before Alice thumped her stick impatiently on the floor. Reluctantly she walked out into the dreary hall. It was the next project on her list. She had in mind an elegant pale green and cream for there.

The door was pulled out of her hands as Livvy flung her hot tear-wracked body into the cool pale pink linen dress Helen had dressed so carefully in after lunch.

'Aunty Helen, you've got to come with me – Mummy's sick.' The girl shook with fright almost too distraught to get the words out.

'Hey it's all right sweetie, calm down.' Bending over she wrapped her arms around Livvy holding her tightly until the small racing heart thumping against her slowed to near normal. In the kitchen she poured some lemonade into the girl's favorite Cinderella glass with its sparkling shoes floating between the layers of plastic. Livvy's small feet dangled from the chair, her red sandals not quite touching the ground. Helen straightened the strap of the girl's light blue sundress from where it had slipped off one bony shoulder, revealing a vulnerable untanned line.

'Now Livvy, tell me what's wrong with Mummy.'

'She's lying on the bed and I can't wake

her up.' The child's eyes shone like wet glass.

'I expect she's just tired and needs a rest, sweetheart. Why don't you and John have tea with me and we'll leave a note for when she wakes up.'

Livvy bounced in the chair while her serious emerald eyes gave Helen the kind of look children frequently bestow on obtuse grown-ups who won't listen properly to them.

'It's not that Aunty Helen, I'm sure it's not. Daddy came home for lunch and shouted at Mummy because we only had sandwiches. He always shouts at her. She told us to stay downstairs but we could still hear them.'

There was little Helen could say in justification of Roger but she had to try. 'Well sometimes grown-ups argue just like you and your friends and then they make up.'

Livvy's too-knowing eyes were scathing of Helen's obvious stupidity and when she spoke it was in the way of a teacher explaining something really simple to a particularly dense student.

'Daddy left in the car you see, so John and I went up to Mummy. She's on the bed and there's red stuff on the pillow. John says it's blood like on TV but I think he's wrong.' Goosebumps stood straight up on Helen's arms hearing the scared uncertainty in Livvy's voice.

'Livvy, I'll phone Uncle Paul and he'll go to help Mummy. Where's John now?' Livvy slipped back into responsible older sister role then, telling Helen how she'd left him playing in their back garden. She had to turn away, not trusting herself to look into those lucid green eyes any longer. Paul listened quietly but it didn't disguise the brief sharp intake of breath at her words. Then the professional routine reassurances took over. Strangely they steadied Helen's jitters – this must be how his patients felt.

Helen made herself behave steadily, as if nothing unusual was going on. With Livvy settled in front of the television she left by the back door. The control went then with panic pumping her legs to run faster than she'd ever done.

For a few seconds she watched as the five-year-old bounced a large red ball against the wall chattering away happily to himself, completely wrapped in his own world. One mention of unlimited cartoons and sweets and his sticky hand slipped into hers. He kept her amused on the walk back with some convoluted story of who did what to whom on the school playground. John was so proud of having started school like his sister – Julie was always telling what a battle she had to get him to change out of his uniform.

The three of them curled up together on the sofa with the two children happily lost in Scooby-Doo. It strained every one of her nerves to breaking point to quietly lift John off her lap when the phone rang. Paul didn't give her a chance to speak.

'She's bad Helen; I've got an ambulance on its way. The police are coming too so keep the children out of the way. I'll call as soon as I know anything. I'm sorry, really, really sorry.' Her head swirled dangerously and the phone gave an empty click in her ear as he hung up.

'Is Mummy all right?' Standing barely inches away Livvy fixed worried eyes on Helen – they were hard to look into and lie but she had to.

'Mummy's a bit poorly but Uncle Paul is taking her to the hospital.' Julie had to pull through this if for no other reason than Helen couldn't fathom how she would tell this sweet girl otherwise. The child nodded, not with conviction but agreeing to go along with the pretence for now.

Helen was suffused with dark sorrow to see Livvy, only nine herself, put her arms around John and speak to him so gently.

'Mummy's not well John, so we're staying here until she's better. Okay?' His round face beamed – Livvy always took care of him. He had cartoons and as many chocolate biscuits as he wanted so it couldn't be too bad.

Digging in the freezer Helen found the remains of a packet of beef burgers stuck down in one corner and a half-used bag of chips that would do for the children's tea. She got the grill heating up and checked to make sure there was milk for them to drink. Then she heard the dragging sticks on the floor.

'What on earth's going on, Helen? We've had no tea this afternoon and when I come to find you, causing myself a lot of pain I might add, I find those Haldon children lying on the best furniture and smearing chocolate all over the place. What on earth were you thinking letting them eat in there?'

God she itched to hit the woman, either that or pop her complacent cocoon by telling her exactly what was going on. Sucking in her anger Helen strived to sound unconcerned. 'Julie's been hurt and Paul's gone with her to the hospital. The children will be here until things are sorted out.' A different type of woman you could ask for help maybe to read them a story but with Alice that would be a wasted effort. 'I'll bring your tea in a minute.' Helen had to watch what she said. This would get around the village soon enough without her help. Alice hobbled away muttering under her breath.

The earlier sun had turned to rain as the weather sought to match the mood of the day. Helen poured water in and out of plastic cups in the steamy bath to amuse John while her mind replayed Paul's last phone call over and over. Julie was in surgery in an attempt to relieve severe brain swelling. Paul hadn't given her any details only saying that the police were looking for Roger. She'd almost told him not be silly with his warnings to lock the doors and not let anyone in but kept her mouth shut. Standing vigil at the hospital was his atonement for laughing at her worries.

Heedless of the tune she joined in John's haphazard rendering of 'Yellow Submarine' seeing full-of-life pictures of Julie dancing to that same song at a long ago school disco playfully boasting how Roger had called to ask her out that weekend. They'd talked so many hours about who would be the first to get a boyfriend and her eyes had glittered with anticipation and glee at being one up on Helen.

Some people you know are rotten inside. Like an apple with a maggoty core it doesn't matter how smooth and shiny the outer peel is. Roger had been charming all right. Ten years older, a grown-up sophisticated man next to the pimply sixteen-year-old boys in class. Julie hadn't stood a chance. The newly qualified lawyer with his racy black sports car had trampled over Helen's tentatively voiced reservations, twisting them into suggestions of jealousy. It hadn't been difficult for him to win over Julie's cautious parents making them believe how lucky she was to have attracted such an impressive man. But luck had had nothing to do with it. Roger had got exactly what he'd planned on – a young easily controlled wife.

'Aunty Helen, that hurts.'

Looking down she saw deep red marks where her nails had absentmindedly dug into the boy's shoulders while her mind seethed with hatred for Roger. John must have suffered for minutes without complaint. 'Oh John, I'm so sorry.' Lifting him out of the cooling water Helen wrapped him in a soft blue towel. Dried off and buttoned into his Spiderman pyjamas the little boy stood patiently as she brushed his silky blonde hair, with each stroke thinking of his poor mother. Tears were only one word away.

Touching his fragile bony head brought to Helen a sudden clarity as to why Julie had been so quiet about her marriage. In a desperate effort to protect her children she'd put up with anything herself. If she'd tried to leave Roger would have ruthlessly tracked her down. The thought was unconscionable that her dearest friend might die because she didn't cook a hot lunch.

The doorbell rang. Helen's arms tightened around John. A paralyzing knot of fear almost closed Helen's throat. 'Stay there.'

On the way down she stopped, pulling back the curtain slightly from the window overlooking the road. In her panic Helen hadn't given Julie's parents a thought but they were standing on her doorstep. As if Roger would have dared to come. He was vicious but not that dumb.

Nobody spoke. Then John noisily tumbled down the stairs and flung himself into his grandfather's arms followed by Livvy who walked silently over to bury her head in her Grandma Sarah's arms.

'Grandma, can you come and read us a bedtime story?' Livvy dragged her grandmother by the hand back up the stairs while chattering non-stop about the bedroom, the amount of chocolate biscuits they'd eaten and the TV they'd watched. The child didn't mention her mother.

Lewis followed Helen into the living room closing the door gently. Her warm hand took his chilled one but the cold transfused from his blood to hers.

'Julie's gone isn't she?'

There was a barely perceptible nod before his head sunk towards his chest. Helen took him to sit on the sofa and went to make tea.

The drinking of it might not help but the action involved in doing something when nothing else was possible might aid her.

'They're in bed. I couldn't tell them yet – let them sleep tonight.' Sarah Williams's thin face had turned almost skeletal with unspeakable hurt. With the half finished cups abandoned Lewis's hoarse words lacerated Helen's heart. 'We were too late; Julie never regained consciousness.'

Guilt pressed like a ton weight on her head making a tumbled stream of apologies pour out. William stilled her virtually incoherent ramblings with one fleeting touch on her arm. 'Don't do this to yourself, Helen, please. We've known for years what was going on but Julie wouldn't let us help. We pleaded with her to leave Roger and come to live with us but she was too afraid of what he'd do. Maybe she would have in time but he didn't give her that did he?'

Paul's blank, pale face appeared in the doorway. The way he stood with his hands clasped together stilled Helen from running into his arms. She listened to his short prepared speech of consolation. It was nothing more that the standard one received by any bereaved patient. She'd heard him do it before. Nothing to indicate this was her best friend he was talking about and the only child of the poor couple holding hands on the sofa, trying desperately to look appreciative while plainly wracked with a pain he seemed not to comprehend.

It froze Helen to the core. By the time she thawed enough later to recognize that he'd known of no other way to cope it was too late. His silence turned her away to a dangerous empty place.

CHAPTER TEN

'Some birds aren't meant to be caged, their feathers are just too bright. And when they fly away, the part of you that knows it was a sin to lock them up, does rejoice, I guess I just miss my friend.'
Shawshank Redemption

As if new curtains and wallpaper were enough to make a person happy. How stupid could she have been?

The sun rose pale-pink in the May sky as Helen sat outside the back door resting her cold bare feet on the flagstones. Anything for some kind of feeling. The mug in her fingers, a present from Julie's last holiday in Wales, held a shrivelled skin of barely drunk coffee. It was way past time to be cooking breakfast but she didn't move. Paul's dark clueless eyes watched from the bedroom window.

Four weeks had passed but the hours blurred into nothingness. One intake of breath was all it took. Then the weighty scent of white lilies filled her senses. Helen could clearly see the flowers stiffly arranged in black wrought iron pedestals, one each side of the altar. One blink of her tear clouded eyes and the polished oak coffin solely adorned with a bunch of yellow tulips picked by the children from Julie's own garden filled Helen's vision. Livvy had painstakingly written her name on the card in her best writing and then guided John's hand to make the letters he didn't yet understand. The awful new black suit Helen had worn – Julie's most hated colour. To Helen that had proved the depth of her cowardice. As teenagers they'd solemnly sworn to dress in bright cheerful colours at the funeral of whoever died first but it had been an easy promise to make in the days when death was for grown-ups. Helen had failed her friend to the very end.

She ached to see Julie's bright eyes in Livvy's rather serious face and hear her in John's laughter but sensibly she'd been kindly but firmly deterred from visiting them yet. They had to be allowed to settle in with their grandparents first without too many reminders but sensible wasn't helping her.

Paul's patience had lasted until Julie's funeral was over. Maybe he was overwhelmed by his own guilt but Helen saw it only as rejection. She was coming to the conclusion that mourning selfishly narrows the soul. The fallacy that it brings people together had to be propagated by those who would like it to be true. It struck her as obscene to relegate

Julie to an occasional reminiscence. She'd tried to move on but the trying was making her angry and so desperately tired.

Sleeplessness plagued her like an invasive virus. Part of her hadn't resented at all the hours spent drinking tea in the kitchen and listening to the clock but Paul's threatened kindness to give her sleeping tablets had driven her to more pretence. He wasn't going to take away her dreams too along with the nightmares.

'Helen it's gone half past seven. Is there any chance I might get some breakfast this morning?' Paul's attempt at humour didn't register. Craving simple comfort all she picked up on was irritation. His preferred calm start to the morning wasn't going to happen yet again today so he gave up and walked away. She didn't turn to notice the worn out slump to his whole self.

From the far end of the table she watched him buttering toast while her own fingers reduced the slice on her plate to cold dry crumbs. Paul wiped a smudge of marmalade from the corner of his mouth, 'Remember I shan't be home for lunch today, I've got a staff meeting.' Helen managed a nod while her insides sighed with relief.

She'd had the idea to get away from the house and go into town but it didn't work.

You don't get away. You take it with you. Crowds of chattering shoppers enjoying the warm day, laughing children in the park, it all emphasized the size of the dark shadow swallowing her up. Thinking she could have lunch in the Red Lion was the craziest mistake. The mere five minutes wait at the bar to order was enough.

She and Julie had stood in exactly the same spot twenty years earlier as a pair of naïve fifteen-year-olds, faces plastered in badly applied make-up, mini-skirts up to their backsides, balanced on borrowed high heels. The barman hadn't even tried to keep a straight face at their request for two small sweet sherries, all they'd ever seen their mothers' drink, laughing out loud and telling them to go home and play. She'd gone red with humiliation but not Julie. Her friend had given the man a look of pure disdain, tossed her newly blonde hair (they'd experimented with a bottle from her mother's bathroom cupboard that morning), pushed her rapidly developing breasts over the counter towards him and then flounced away. How they'd laughed when they got outside before wiping off the worst of the make-up and heading straight for the Wimpy Bar where they were supposed to be in the first place.

As she put her old blue Mini in gear and pulled out of the car park Roger's poster, the edges curled up and brown, mocked her from the pay booth. It made her drive angrily home and screech to a halt on the gravel inches before hitting the garage doors. Her pale hands tightly clenched the wheel and shook.

Even the safety of the house couldn't stop her heart thumping loudly. Answering the phone her fingers twisted the wire into tangled knots as a too well recognized voice slipped into her hearing. Hang up. That's what she should do.

'Is that you Helen?'

Polite. She had to be polite. 'Good afternoon Simon. How are you?' Normal, cool.

'I'm okay but I read an article in this morning's newspaper about a police search for Roger Haldon and saying what had happened to Julie. I'm so sorry. Why didn't you let me know?'

'It never occurred to us you'd be that concerned – after all you only met her once.' Helen's guilty defensiveness flooded through until it took very little to imagine condemnation on Simon's part.

'I only thought...' What had he thought and why did he think she cared? 'I do understand...' That did it.

'No you don't understand. No one does or even tries to. If I hadn't been so pigheaded about good manners and not treading on people's feelings Julie might still be alive. I knew Roger was violent and mean, I've always known, but I didn't do anything about it. You have absolutely no idea how that makes me feel.'

In a few well-chosen sentences Simon cleverly insinuated into her mind the very idea that had been hovering at the edges of her brain. 'I'm sure you did what you could. It's always easier to see these things afterwards. Anyway Paul was her doctor so why not let him share any blame?' She was so ripe for sympathy it wasn't funny.

The phone remained in her hand long after he'd hung up. Helen had no concept of why she'd willingly agreed to Simon visiting again any more than someone does when they've been hypnotized by a shiny swinging watch into doing something out of character.

She was smart enough to turn her back on Alice's sharp eyes over the dinner table before casually mentioning Simon's call while dishing up the chicken casserole. The burst of undisguised pleasure in Paul's face sent a guilty shiver down her spine.

Rightly or wrongly the Thursday morning sunshine flooding through the filmy white curtains lightened Helen's battered heart. After weeks of food prepared under sufferance – giving no joy either in the cooking or eating - Helen hummed softly as the kitchen counters disappeared under racks of pies, rolls, scones and of course one of the dark chocolate cakes Simon loved.

Her easier mood allowed her the latitude to slap Paul's hand playfully away as he grabbed a fresh biscuit from the growing pile. His eyes betrayed joy at a respite from her recent gloom and a small surge of affection impelled Helen to plant a warm kiss on his cheek. The arousal in both their bodies as he pulled her hips to meet his was obvious and the disconcerting thing was that she found herself not minding. Helen didn't want to think too much. It was a little scary how badly she needed Paul to almost force himself on her right then, to create a memory that would fortify her when Simon arrived. But it was too much to expect. His slight pulling away shouldn't really have been a surprise.

'Let's go to bed early tonight darling.' Tonight. Too late.

'What's wrong with now?'

Paul's face flushed bright scarlet, 'Are you mad? What if my parents walk in or somebody comes to the back door?' The rush of desire inflaming her died, doused by his cold sense. Her hands dropped away.

'Forget it. Anyway I ought to clear this mess up. Maybe later.' They both knew there wouldn't be a later. Helen strived to feel sorry for him as a confusion of longing and shame contorted his features. The knowledge of his love should have been enough.

CHAPTER ELEVEN

'Love truth and pardon error.'
Voltaire (1694-1778)

Insomnia is an alluring habit. Those hours solely hers. They belong to her and the church clock in the cool dark-laden night. She longs to sit by the window closer to the stars but instead lays perfectly still on the freshly ironed yellow sheets as far away from Paul as possible. The frightening truth Helen desperately avoids acknowledging is that what she really craves is to tiptoe silently along the corridor to Simon's room and slip into an unknown world. Tomorrow morning over muesli and toast this remembrance will resemble nothing more than an imaginatively written magazine story but in the seductive black night it appears only too possible. Daylight will expose the idea as stupid, illicit, vulgar and immoral but...

It had taken ten minutes. That was all.

Ten counted minutes from the time he strolled into the house, tanned and loose haired. No one else in sight; Paul delayed by an awkward patient and Alice and Jack having tea at the vicarage. They'd exchanged regular words of desultory polite conversation and commented on the garden. God she'd been so easy. Maybe he was lying in bed right now laughing. But she couldn't bear to believe that.

One simple expression of his sorrow about Julie, one fleeting touch of his hand on hers and that had been it. Helen's tears had poured out with none of the restraint everyone else expected. He'd put comforting arms around her and then they'd kissed under the old gnarled apple tree, how much more clichéd was it possible to get?

To think of your husband's son this way was sick. That was so obvious. Any normal rational person would think so and that was exactly what Helen was, everyone who knew her would tell you that. She'd never done anything outrageous or illogical in her whole life; been a quiet, obedient child, dutiful daughter and loving wife. The worst thing she'd done was smoke a single cigarette with Julie one morning at the school bus stop but even that she'd choked on and never tried again.

Perspective was slowly returning, forcing its way into her dream. And that's all it ever could or should be.

If anyone had asked the next morning Helen would have sworn she hadn't slept at all but the alarm clock's clanging ring definitely woke her. Her gritty tired eyes focused on Paul lying peacefully beside her, his mouth half-open, relaxed and trusting. Had he woken then and watched her getting ready there still wouldn't have been any obvious signs for him to see and question. Maybe she took a little longer in the shower, bothered to use the hairdryer, took a shade more care in choosing clothes for the day, and added a touch of discreet lipstick, but nothing in the way of a red flag except to a very observant bull.

Her sandals moved soundlessly on the carpet but a step before the turn in the stairs Helen stopped as Simon's voice drifted up the stairs. Why she didn't carry on down was a question she couldn't have answered.

'Hello darling, sorry to call this early but it's my only chance. You were so right. Mind you I had to close my eyes and imagine it was you I was kissing. I'm not going to be able to keep this up for long. No, not that...' His cruel sensuous laugh made Helen's stomach churn. 'I'll just tease her a bit more and then leave. A few more weeks and she'll definitely be ready when I come back. I'm going to get so much pleasure telling my precious so-called father his wife's nothing but a slut.'

Surely she'd be sick all over the carpet, or rush down and rip him apart but neither happened. She wasn't even shaking only filled instead with an eerie freezing cold leaving her completely numb. A few more softly spoken words and he hung up the phone.

Helen stayed motionless until he'd disappeared from sight. No doubt he was checking out what was new in the garden to make fawning comments on later. Leadenly Helen walked down to the kitchen looking around at it all as if in a stranger's house.

'Helen, what the devil are you doing? Where's all the smoke coming from?'

Why was Paul so mad? It hardly registered when he roughly snatched the flaming bacon pan from her hand, throwing it into the sink and dowsing it with a wet towel. The cool morning air from the flung open windows hit her prickling skin.

'Are you trying to burn the house down?'

An intense stinging sensation beat a path through Helen as the nerves in her hand finally acknowledged the reddening palm where she'd gripped the handle long after it was screaming hot. Frigid water hitting the surface layer of blistering skin startled her to tears but she couldn't pull away from Paul's firm hold. 'Keep it there until I get back with some bandages, all right?' She couldn't answer for fear of screaming. He was all gentleness after that, drying her hand carefully, spraying on a soothing antiseptic and efficiently bandaging it. Pouring them both some tea he gave her two aspirins to take and sat with her, asking nothing.

Some last remnant of sense kept her mouth wisely sealed shut on an almost crippling urge to confess. Revealing her own shameful behaviour would destroy Paul's belief in Simon and he didn't deserve that. She wasn't the only one to have suffered these last few months. Her selfishness must stop.

'Hello, anybody around yet?' Simon's breezy voice echoed around the hall. Paul shifted to get up but Helen's good hand stopped him. Without his presence she'd fall apart.

'What's happened? Are you all right, Helen?' Burying her head in Paul's shoulder allowed her to avoid Simon's searching eyes and give in to the excruciating weariness sweeping through her. The concise version of her accident Paul spouted almost convinced her – it sounded amazingly truthful. 'I'm taking Helen upstairs to rest, get whatever you want and I'll see to Mother and Dad in a while.'

Tucked into the cool sheets she ached for Paul to stay but the reasoning was weak to her own ears; the truth of not wanting to be in bed and vulnerable impossible to voice. He wasn't to know his kindly meant promise for Simon to check on her during the morning was the very last thing she wanted.

89

'He needn't bother, all I want is to sleep.'

Naturally that brought out the professional doctor side of him along with a slightly condescending pat of her hand. 'Now don't be silly Helen, someone has to make sure you're okay and I won't have time. I'll be back at lunchtime but don't you dare get up until I say so all right?'

Closing her eyes to the light was worse as ugly unbidden pictures filled the emptiness. At some point her body must have closed down, deciding for her that she'd had enough.

'Are you awake Helen? I've brought you some coffee.'

With a soft groan she twisted away from his concern. If she didn't answer perhaps he'd go away leaving her in the closest thing to peace she was likely to find. The chair scraped on the polished floorboards as he dragged it over closer to the bed. The evil words that had flowed earlier from his mouth ran around her head. The pain in her hand was nothing in comparison. A torrent of sympathy poured from Simon's untrustworthy lips. It made the tiny knot of anger lodged in the pit of her stomach multiply into a huge mass of clenching fury. Tucking the fluffy cream blanket in around her exposed throat Helen sat up searing furious eyes into his apparently loving face.

'Get out of my room and out of my house. I don't care what excuse you make to Paul but you'd better make it good so as not to hurt him anymore. Go back to your precious girlfriend and don't worry – I don't want your pawing hands on me again any more than you want them there. You sicken me almost as much as I do myself. Paul didn't abandon you, you've had a good home and family so what's your problem that you need to do this to him?'

Disbelief replaced by resignation flitted over his face. There was no attempt to defend his actions. Very slowly and deliberately Simon stood and returned the chair to its usual spot against the wall. One step away from opening the door he turned back, the look on his face impossible to decipher. It almost resembled deep sadness. She had to look away.

'I know what you heard and I'm not going to make any excuses that you'd be wise not to trust anyway. In one way you're right but... One day I hope you'll know differently.' He walked away.

A gush of hot liquid fell on the clean covers as her trembling hand finally lost control of the cup. She rubbed in vain at the rapidly spreading brown stain and then all that was left was to lie there and think.

Being quiet in the kitchen wasn't something

Paul was good at, banging around as he tried to find what he was looking for. He could never remember where anything was if it wasn't a medical instrument. At least it gave her time to pull herself together and try not to look too miserable. He came in carrying a plate of badly cut sandwiches and a mug of tea; the sight of damp tomato oozing through the bread churned her stomach. After ten years didn't he know she hated tomato in a sandwich more than just about anything?

'Shame about Simon's father isn't it?' All she could do was look concerned and hope for some further hint. 'I said to call and let us know how he's doing. Heart trouble at that sort of age always needs to be taken seriously but hopefully they caught it in time.' Simon had chosen wisely. Quietly murmured agreement was all Paul required of her. Thankfully he went to see to Alice and Jack so the offending lunch could be wrapped in a napkin and hidden away in her bedside table. She wasn't hungry anyway.

By four o'clock Helen managed to wriggle into some old sweatpants and a loose T-shirt before thinking drove her totally mad. This was one of those days when Helen didn't know how she was going to bear life without her friend. If she lay down for a while and rested, the sensible option, she wouldn't get up again today and then Simon would have won.

The main achievement of the evening was to survive Alice and Jack joining them after dinner to watch TV and tolerate it until news time. Finally then her conscience allowed her to use the pain from her heavily bandaged hand as an excuse to go to bed. Nothing she said deterred Paul from joining her, tolerating an excess of his kindness tonight was hopefully today's final punishment.

What would it be like to roll over, snake her body around his like a spoon? She wondered if his ordinary normality could become part of her or if touching would be too much. He didn't speak so maybe her contrived steady breathing had fooled him. Escaping with her thoughts into dark night allowed a brief respite from guilt. She was grateful for anything.

CHAPTER TWELVE

'We deceive ourselves when we fancy that only weakness needs support. Strength needs it far more.'
Madame Swetchine,
The Writings of Madame Swetchine

Systematically Helen cleaned, gardened, ran around after Alice and presented the façade of a loving wife. She did it well enough to almost believe in it herself. Through the unusually intense summer heat she surged with a feverish energy.

The way she ferociously scraped at the living room walls hinted at some purpose Paul didn't understand; his tentative suggestion that she might be overdoing it was laughed at, sort of kindly. Strands of damp hair stuck to the back of her neck and trickles of sweat ran down between her shoulder blades pooling at the base of her spine as the glaring sun poured in through the open windows. Occasionally she'd stop a moment, wave and say hello to a friend walking by but most of the time her concentration was fixed. To her own reasoning all this activity was surely healthier than Prozac. There was huge motivation to finish before the elaborate tea party she had planned out for Alice and Jack's 60th wedding anniversary. Alice's raised eyebrows when she'd announced redecorating plans was more than enough to spur Helen on.

It was a struggle not to resent the clock striking half past twelve; cleaning up and fixing lunch were nothing but annoying interruptions. It would have to be salad again seeing as it was too hot for anything else. Of course Alice would pointedly re-chop everything into smaller pieces and chew indigestion tablets all afternoon but that couldn't be helped. Downing a couple of glasses of icy cold water first at the sink, Helen joined them at the table, putting on a friendly expression and hiding her work roughened hands in her lap.

Alice finished her meal, put her knife and fork to rest on the plate and cleared her throat. 'I've got some good news'. Helen glimpsed a fearful glance from Jack to his wife and shivered before any more words were even spoken. 'I spoke to Simon this morning and invited him to our anniversary. He was pleased to be asked and said as his father is better he wouldn't miss it for anything.' The room closed ominously in around Helen as her mother-in-law turned in her direction. Alice managed to gloat and warn with the same look.

'He's such a considerate young man. I'm to tell you Helen that he'll stay at the pub so as not to give you any extra work. I tried to insist on him staying here but he wouldn't give in. He's travelling down on Sunday but he'll only be able to stay a couple of days because it's a hectic time of year in his business.'

The conversation revolved on around the planned party. Helen thought no one noticed her reticence, too wrapped up in her own jumbled thoughts to see Jack's worried pale blue eyes resting sympathetically on her.

The next few days slipped mercilessly by. Time never seemed to go slowly when you wanted it to. At least the full days of decorating and cooking gave Helen's fatigued body permission to sink into an immediate deep sleep every night. She couldn't really have held her breath all day Sunday but it felt that way. In desperation she took Alice to church, something she rarely did, partly in the hope that that some little nugget of peace might worm its way in. All it achieved was to give more opportunity for the panicking ideas filling her brain to expand their territory.

Minute by minute the afternoon dragged by convincing Helen that Simon was toying with her too aware of how she'd be dreading his arrival. He understood far too much. Finally, when her nerves were down to the last possible shred of normality, there was a polite late evening phone call announcing his arrival but refusing Paul's offer of supper or a drink.

Helen touched a hand gingerly to her temple giving the suggestion of a headache, 'I'm going on to bed, I've a lot to do tomorrow.' She couldn't examine too closely what made her put to one side her usual faded blue cotton nightdress and reach instead for a silky peach one, her last birthday present from Julie. The ease in which it slipped on made Helen pause briefly in front of the mirror. The only other time she'd tried it the sight of the myriad of bumps emphasized by the thin material led to its being shoved to the back of the drawer. At least one good thing had come out of the last few months worry and hard work. That brought a quick smile to her lips, the first for days.

Moving towards the window Helen opened it enough to soak in the warm breeze but loud voices from the pub filled the air. It emphasized how close he was and how wrong she was to care about that. Returning to the bathroom Helen changed. The worn out comfortable nightdress suited more the person she needed to be.

Monday morning and more acting. Only two days and she could relax again. There was no good looking beyond that. Simon's role as perfect grandson was enhanced by offering to take Alice and Jack into town for lunch and some shopping, his only direct words to Helen were shared pleasantly over breakfast as he laughingly promised to keep them out of the way all day. Her own part as loving wife, caring daughter-in-law and friendly quasi stepmother wrung out Helen's best performance ever. If Oscars were given to amateurs she'd have had no competition.

As they gathered on the patio after dinner a casual observer would easily have been fooled. An elderly couple, together for most of a lifetime, sits close and talks amiably. A middle-aged man, his arm gently resting on the back of his wife's chair occasionally leans over to whisper in her ear and kiss her cheek softly. In a half-darkened corner of the patio, shadowed by a cascade of sweetly fragrant white roses, sits a younger man, and as his open kind face turns towards the others he recounts amusing stories about some of his customers.

With the darkness moving in Simon is left alone, his coffee long since cold in the cup. He appears not to notice the creeping chill in the air as the warm summer evening fades. Drained by the effort he'd put into the day he allows his eyes to close for a few brief minutes.

Five o'clock. Helen quickly silences the

alarm. Pulling on an old denim skirt she's surprised to need a belt, something she's avoided wearing for years. A rather worn-out pink flowery shirt and white sandals will do until later. The rubber band in her hand is tossed down on the dressing table replaced by the sensation of newly grown loose hair around her shoulders.

There is something about the silent darkened house Helen likes. For a moment there are no problems or responsibilities more pressing than whether her cakes will rise or not. After putting the kettle on she unlocks the back door bending down over the step to pick up the milk bottles. As her hands touch the cold beaded dew on the glass they fall to her sides. In a patio chair someone is sleeping.

Tiptoeing into the pale morning light the trace of a smile curls across her face. In defiance of any good judgment she can't resist reaching out to push a lock of gleaming jet-black hair away from Simon's forehead. Intense golden eyes like a feral cat return her stare and the shock unbalances Helen. Stumbling backwards only his hand on her arm stops her from falling. With no conscious knowledge of movement her face ends up mere inches from his, so close that his quickened breath warms her skin. They don't speak a word. She can't and he wisely resists.

Mixing scones is easy; she's made them hundreds of times over the years so her mind can afford to wander. Thank goodness the weather is dry so people will be able to sit outside as the living room's bound to fill up quickly. Paul will need to get a couple more pints of milk when he gets home. Simon offered but she won't let him to do anything. Helen has to push from memory yet again how badly she'd longed for him to kiss her.

The amusement hovering around his mouth when she'd pushed him away had made her want to slap him for his unspoken certainty that there would be another time.

A little more milk and a few sultanas, roll the dough, cut them out, and they're ready for the oven. The timer goes off and out come two perfect chocolate cakes to cool on wire racks waiting to be iced. Her body aches with the physical effort of being held together and functioning. She can get through this. He'll leave and she and Paul will be all right. They have to be. She can't imagine any other life, which may or may not be a reason to stay in this one.

Making endless pots of tea, pouring sherry, cutting cake, arranging the overflow of flowers in anything that will hold them, watching Alice hold court while Jack sits quietly at her side. The day blurs happily away. Paul's welcome compliments on her new pale green dress. The voiceless unsought for ones from Simon from his admiring eyes. Finally she stands at the kitchen sink with the shoes kicked off her tired sore feet, finishing the dishes.

The cooler evening air draws Helen out into the garden. Peacefully she breathes in the relaxing scent of lavender before hesitant footsteps echo behind her on the path. Her heart thumps uncontrollably knowing whom she both dreads and longs for it to be.

CHAPTER THIRTEEN

*'You see what power is – holding someone else's
fear in your hand and showing it to them.'*
Amy Tan (1952–)

'Ah there you are Helen.'

Jack's kind smile was hesitant as if unsure
how it would be received.

'I didn't get the chance to thank you properly earlier for all you did my dear. We had
a wonderful time and I know it meant a lot to
Alice – even if she didn't say so. Actually
she'd like to have a word with you so I think
she probably wants to thank you herself.
Would you mind going in to see her?'

Someone was watching over her wild im-
pulses after all. 'Of course not Jack, and it
was my pleasure to give the party for you
both.' Anyone living with Alice for sixty
years deserved more than a drink and a slice
of cake in her opinion but....

'Come in and close the door.'

Presumably her mother-in-law didn't
want anyone else to overhear her being nice.
Right now all Helen wanted was to get out
of her crumpled dress and into a cool
shower but she sat obediently in Jack's usual

chair determined to be pleasant.

'I'm not planning on wasting my breath on thanks, you got more than enough of those. Someone has to say something to you and apparently the only one around here with open eyes is me.' The stream of malevolence continued. 'I'm talking about Simon of course. You fooled us so well last time you even had me convinced I'd made a mistake. But you slipped up this morning by forgetting I often don't sleep well. I was making an early cup of tea and saw the pair of you clearly from the kitchen window. You're nothing better than a common slut.' The words were spat out filling the room with hatred. 'It's my duty as Paul's mother to tell him. He deserves to know what's going on.'

Helen so badly wanted to slap Alice's smug features she had to shove her trembling hands under her sweat soaked thighs. Standing up to her mother-in-law was her only chance as the woman always mocked any sign of weakness. She sat straighter in the chair, stared challengingly into Alice's eyes.

'That's fine, go ahead and tell him but he won't believe you. He loves me and knows that I love him. Do you really think he'll fall for your stupid story? He's not easily going to believe anything against Simon either – surely you realize that by now?'

Alice's skin was a frightening shade of purple, her breath loud and laboured. 'You little bitch. You may think you'll get away with this but you won't. I know my son better than you do and he won't...'

The door banged open against the wall. 'What on earth's all this yelling about? And what won't I do Mother?' Alice's mouth clamped shut as the furious anger of a minute ago visibly drained away. Helen pushed sticky strands of hair back away from her flaming hot face and said nothing. Let her make the first move.

'Shouting? I'm sure we weren't, were we Helen dear?' She could only shake her head in agreement and wait to see what came next. 'We were just talking about whether you might want to move from the village one day, Helen seemed to think you may and I said it was a ridiculous idea.'

Paul looked from one to the other, searching their faces for the unsaid. Helen stood and grinned as falsely as she ever had done. 'It was probably a silly idea. Good night Alice, and congratulations again. You and Jack are certainly a wonderful example to us, aren't they Paul?' Turn it around. She can't get out of that one.

Paul hated arguments. Relief filled his eyes almost to the brink of tears. 'Yes they are. And Mother you were right, I've no intention of leaving, I don't know what Helen was thinking of.' The kind way he spoke made it clear she was forgiven for her part in the upset.

Tonight the peach silk would be a necessity. Any probing questions and she'd be likely to say something stupid. Alice had been stopped for now but if ever anyone had been sent a warning this was one. There wouldn't be any more hints. Next time would be too late. She must remember that phone call. How could she overhear wicked words like those and think of Simon as anything more than an arrogant, sly young man determined to cause trouble? It was time to stop behaving like a silly teenager.

Paul wasn't a complicated man. His job was satisfying. He loved his wife and his parents and was at his happiest when life was peaceful. The sight of Helen lying on the bed, the golden material clinging seductively to her lightly tanned skin and her hair, now attractively shoulder length, fanned gently across the pillow was enough to banish any lingering questions he might've had. Reaching for her she opened herself to him with a rare abandonment, sinking into his passion.

Did other women do this? Would it be better to be fought with rather than given into so very willingly? As she moved automatically under him the thoughts cascaded like a rushing waterfall and the remaining moonlight caught the silvery remnant of dried tears on Helen's cheeks. He didn't notice.

Helen's hands rested on the stainless steel of the sink while a welcome chill shivered its way down through her. Hard rain pulsed into the parched grass outside, beating its way into the cracked dry earth. After endless weeks of lazy blue skies it was strange to look out onto the grey morning but it suited her mood. It was a returning to ordinary life.

It occurred to her that things were almost better than they'd been before Sarah's fateful letter. Oh sometimes Paul smiled his quirky smile at her latest interests, the yoga classes and aromatherapy, but it was an understanding humour. Today was Thursday so one of her days for the garden design course she'd started and truly loved. The other night they had actually managed a conversation about starting a family without Paul going on the defensive so that was progress. The dark guilty corner though in her life that never went away belonged to Julie. There were days it verged on overwhelming but then her friend's strong presence came through and a smiling reminiscence would cheer Helen's sadness.

The way she saw it she'd got her mid-life crisis over with early.

Hours, days, weeks, months, they all slip by and many Sundays Helen would look back and wonder where the previous week had gone – joining the pool of unnoticed time.

'Sweetheart, what do you think about asking Simon here for Christmas?'

Before Helen can answer Alice speaks, her words aimed towards Paul but her dark eyes focused on Helen. 'I don't think that's wise. His parents may think you're trying to lure him away from them. Why don't you leave it until next year?'

Childishly the interference irritates Helen, enough to make her speak before thinking, always unwise. The idea of Alice protecting her from herself is ridiculous. 'I think it's a great idea darling. He doesn't have to accept but that way he'd know you'd like him to be part of our family too.' Encouraged by one of her most radiant smiles Paul reaches for the phone. Behind his back Helen gives Alice a triumphant grin and receives her reward in his happy smile when he finishes talking.

'Well that's wonderful. He hesitated a bit at first but I managed to get out of him that he'd really like to bring his girlfriend along to meet us. That's all right isn't it Helen?'

She can't say no to him now, swallowing hard to push down the nausea. Alice is scrutinizing her for any betrayal of emotion. In her best warm self-assured voice Helen told Paul what fantastic news it was.

Indifference from a distance was one thing but this was something else.

CHAPTER FOURTEEN

'Where is there dignity unless there is honesty.'
Cicero (106BC – 43BC)

Helen covertly admired Anna's snakelike legs emerging from a very short red garment barely deserving the name of 'a skirt.' Naturally her pale cream cashmere sweater clung to all the right places as well. Perfectly manicured nails in matching post-box red caught the light as she idly stroked immaculate straight long blonde hair – a fact she was plainly aware of.

The whole effect of Anna's appearance was to make Helen feel old and dowdy; the new blue dress she'd thought looked great in the shop last week now seemed provincial and boring. She examined her own nail-bitten, work-stained hands; gardening wasn't exactly conducive to good grooming. The new hairdresser she'd recklessly tried had got a bit carried away, why did they always think when you said a bit shorter and more modern you wanted this kind of drastic change? The highlights had glowed prettily in the salon but now gave an almost orangey tinge to her hair in certain lights.

Not much of a confidence booster.

Of course Simon's stick thin girlfriend only politely toyed with the slice of iced Christmas cake on her plate. The remaining few crumbs on her own made it obvious why Anna's dress size was in single digits and hers... At the moment the girl was listening to Alice's monologue with apparent fascination but she could probably do that with her eyes shut being a TV presenter. Not obviously Simon's type, but then who was she to know what his 'type' was?

Paul's eyebrows had lifted nearly through his head when the pair arrived earlier. She hadn't seen him so disconcerted for a long time. Their speculations beforehand had pictured a nice, quietly spoken Scottish girl but then Mata Hari here had arrived. With her cut glass accent and designer clothes Anna projected a distinctly amused air at spending the holidays in the wilds of remote Cornwall.

Now they were being studied like animals in a zoo while Simon merely gave that sexy laid-back smile of his, underpinned by a twist of self-satisfaction. He was definitely enjoying this. It was going to be a very long three days.

'The cake is delicious, Helen.'

How would she know?

'Thank you.'

If Simon's not careful she'll wipe that

supercilious smirk off his face.

'So Helen, what else do you do anything apart from run this beautiful house and cook divinely?'

Cow.

'I'm studying for a garden design qualification at the moment.'

She kept her fingers metaphorically crossed that it sounded better than the two days a week at the local college it really was.

'Oh how interesting. You and Simon have something in common then. He's always messing around in the dirt too.'

A brief flicker of sympathy flashed across Simon's previously inscrutable face before he draped his arm around Anna's shoulder and nuzzled her face playfully. If Helen had to watch much more of this she'd throw up.

'I must get on and clear up. Dinner will be at eight and we'll be going to the midnight service. Obviously you're more than welcome to join us.'

Anna's glossy lips twitched humorously, 'Thank you but I don't know what Simon has planned.' The blatant glance she threw in his direction made it crystal clear to everyone what she thought he might have in mind as an alternative to Christmas carols. His silent disapproval, which manifested itself so subtly, wasn't hard for Helen to recognize – she'd seen it enough times before.

'Thanks, I'd like that, we always go at

home. Anna can do what she likes.' That didn't go down well. The beautiful face wasn't quite as lovely with a sulky turned down mouth.

Helen pushed down the little smirk of satisfaction threatening to spring out of its good mannered coil. On this night of universal peace and goodwill it wasn't very kind to laugh at Anna shivering in a smart white suit, her skin turning an unattractive shade of pale purple but some things it just wasn't possible to help. For the unheated granite church layers of sensible warm clothes, hats and gloves weren't only preferable but essential. Helen's own cherry red coat might be years old but it kept her distinctly cosy and didn't look too bad with the new matching velvet hat she'd found and pulled down over the offending hair. Thank goodness Paul had given her his present early, the knee length sheepskin boots meant her toes could happily wriggle around instead of shrivelling up with the cold.

For a brief hour she found some measure of peace inspired by the familiar tunes and rows of flickering candles. It buoyed her up, and as they emerged into the crisp starry night the bell tower behind was lit up like a beacon. Paul had bravely offered to walk on ahead with the half-frozen Anna promising her a large whisky for her tolerance. It was the only suggestion to bring a smile to her face the whole evening. After greeting some friends that left Helen to stroll back down the path beside Simon.

His gloved hand lightly touched her arm. 'Happy Christmas Helen.' She waited for another double-edged remark but none came and her previous anger at him faded away. Her throat seized up, too full to do more than return his good wishes. Simon tucked her hand into the crook of his elbow – she decided he probably wasn't aware of stroking it absentmindedly as they walked.

Why didn't the woman tell her she was a vegetarian before Helen placed a golden brown sixteen-pound turkey down on the table for Paul to carve? Last night's cheese pasta had been sheer luck. Of course Anna graciously insisted that the vegetables were plenty for her to eat but Helen felt terrible. Simon hadn't been pleased; the whispered conversation about Anna's claim to have mentioned the fact didn't stay whispered. The rest of the day turned into a long drawn out form of torture. Alice complained about everything from the colour and itchy texture of the new cardigan Helen had spent ages choosing for her to the fact that Simon was leaving too soon. It was hard to believe Paul was naïve enough to suggest they play their usual Christmas game of charades as though he didn't pick up at all on the atmosphere. All he received in reply were disdainful looks.

Eleven o'clock and she'd finally managed to get rid of them all, turning down Paul's offer of help with the dishes. He was absolutely worn out with trying to keep up the façade of Yuletide cheer and she was too tired to support him in it any longer. It hurt to see him trying so hard. With everything done she put off going to bed, pouring a glass of the red wine left from dinner and sitting at the kitchen table, her usual thinking place – it had absorbed a lot recently.

'Only alcoholics drink alone, so do you mind if I join you?' Simon's low, molten voice broke the silence. She was drawn to his striking face, lit only by the small lamp on the counter. 'Help yourself.'

He took a large swallow before clearing his throat awkwardly. 'I'm sorry about today Helen, really sorry.' Her attempted protest that it was all right was stopped by his next words. 'I shouldn't have brought Anna here. I don't know why I did... No that's a lie and I'm sick of lying to you. I do know. I did it to spite you.' She ought to leave. The game playing was starting again.

Putting down his glass he scooped her hands into his, stilling her trembling fingers. 'What I said on the phone I didn't mean, it's complicated.' The piercing golden eyes bored into her keeping Helen in a bewitched form of silence.

'Before I met Sarah and Paul I was very bitter about the whole adoption. I wanted to hate them and pay them back for hurting me.' It came across as more bewildered than angry.

'Why does it matter so much if your parents are such good people?'

There was that change again, the one he just couldn't hide, with her hands roughly dropped to the table as he leapt to his feet. 'You just don't get it do you?' He plainly couldn't believe her incomprehension. 'The fact that they're fantastic isn't the point. Finding out that Paul was an admired doctor with a successful practice didn't endear him to me even before we met. I wanted dumping me to have ruined his life too.'

Simon thrust his face so close his angry breath threatened to consume her making her heart race like crazy. Helen beat down fear striving to make her reply calming and simple. 'But can't you see this obsession is destroying you and hurting the rest of us that you're dragging in there as well?'

The effort to get back in control was nearly beyond Simon. 'I know all that and I'm fighting it. I was too mad to see the truth and when Anna told me Paul had a much younger wife and came up with the idea that seducing you would upset him more than anything else I could do, well, I couldn't see straight.'

Bitch. 'What was in this for her?'

His answer was unexpected.

'Well we've been going out off and on for a while and she's been angling to get me to marry her. She must have thought "helping" me with this would do the trick.'

Before she could prevent it Helen laughed. 'But why on earth would she want to do that?'

The unplanned insult brought the sparkle back to Simon's eyes. 'Believe it or not, in Ardmore I'm considered a good catch. My family has a small estate you see and, adopted or not, I'm still the heir. Anna has this vision of herself as the laird's wife lording it over the downtrodden peasants.'

Helen blushed furiously. 'I didn't mean to be rude. She's just so...'

'I'm just so what?' Anna swept into the room in a cloud of perfume and filmy white satin, her icy blue eyes sawing through them both. 'Go on say it. You've been longing to ever since I got here. For God's sake Helen, open your eyes. He's nothing but a lying cheat telling us both whatever story he thinks we want to hear. If you're stupid enough to fall for his tales that's your fault. I don't know why I allowed myself to be persuaded to come to this god-forsaken hole in the first place.'

Languidly stretching her sleek body she yawned loudly as if they weren't worth expounding any more energy on. 'And by the way Simon, you can keep your grubby little inheritance, I've got bigger fish to fry than you. Much bigger.'

On her way out Anna landed a bull's eye with her parting shot, 'Oh and Helen just so you know, he's a lousy lover who hasn't got a clue how to please a real woman – of course that may suit you. I can't imagine Simon will have much in the way of competition from that dolt of a husband of yours.'

Behind her she left not only a cloying trail of perfume but also even more questions.

CHAPTER FIFTEEN

'I think there is choice possible to us at any moment, as long as we live. But there is no sacrifice. There is a choice, and the rest falls away. Second choice does not exist. Beware of those who talk about sacrifice.'
Muriel Rukeyser, The Life of Poetry

Helen groaned and rolled over, her sticky half-closed eyes protesting at the unwelcome sunshine probing its way in. A dull headache caused by too much indifferent wine hung around her edges and her mouth needed a good scrub to clear the sour taste away. Then her memory woke up.

This time it had been totally her choice. It would be easy to place the guilt at the bottom of a wine glass but dishonest. The reverberation of Anna's bedroom door as she slammed it shut had reached all the way downstairs. Simon wouldn't be sharing her room tonight. One ironic raised eyebrow was his only response followed by another deep swallow of wine.

Helen had stood to leave, well that's what she'd told herself but had the intention ever been there? With one finger she'd touched his cheek, rubbing the end of the day shadow of dark stubble lingering on his warm skin. At that point she could still have changed her mind and come to her senses but instead she'd slid onto his lap. Before he touched her Simon had questioned with his eyes. Remaining there was her answer.

Just because they hadn't committed adultery in the dictionary sense didn't stop fat hot tears from rolling down and soaking the pillow. Paul would surely smell the stench of betrayal when he woke. And what had she got from it? A few minutes of breathless passion, no promises, no explanations – nothing.

'Hey darling, what's wrong?' The concern on his face made Helen want to scream with guilt. Make the madness go away and her old quiet life return. 'Headache? I'll get some aspirin.' Two little white tablets weren't going to do it. Paul let in the clear fresh air bringing a touch of reality to her skewed senses. Nobody had seen them. She could beat this as long as Simon was sent away for good this time. How she was going to achieve that Helen had still to work out.

Taking a glass of water from his hand she listened as Paul answered the phone. The frown lines deepened on his forehead as the muscles moved from relaxed to worried in a matter of seconds. The last few months had taught her a lot about her husband meaning she wasn't so easy to fool these days.

'I've got to go out for a while.' He couldn't quite look directly at her.

'But you're not on duty today, James is, can't he manage?'

'It's not a patient.' All the time he spoke Paul was dressing, any signs of concern well disguised.

She had no right to be fierce and accusatory but it didn't stop her, 'Why are you being secretive? You haven't got another ex-wife hidden away have you?' Helen couldn't take her eyes from his taut closed mouth as he carefully finished tying his shoelaces watching for any little sign. Paul's cool professional expression slotted neatly into place then.

'Look darling it's nothing serious. I'll only be an hour or so. Why don't you stay in bed and rest, it'll do you good.' He took some money from the drawer where they always kept some extra and placed it in his wallet. Who was she to question any secrets he might keep from her anyway?

Keep busy, that was what she did best. All the familiar things, showering, dressing and cooking breakfast soothed. She took Alice and Jack in a nicely laid tray; neatly steering around questions about Paul's whereabouts. As to Anna and Simon they were definitely something to be left well alone. Helen sat down with a quiet cup of tea lost in thought.

'Good morning, I'm getting expert at guessing where to find you aren't I? Of course you don't make it very challenging seeing as it's usually here or the garden.' Her stomach flipped with a sickening lurch at hearing Simon's totally casual laugh. Before she could react his arms were around her and soft kisses planted on her lips and neck. The sensation of his skin against hers was too intoxicating for sense; at that precise second of existence she could no more have retreated than willingly die.

'I knew I'd catch you filthy pair sooner or later.' Alice's violent fury filled the room. 'Oh, Jack complained that I was stirring things up just to cause trouble but I knew I was right.' Simon stilled Helen's effort to move away by holding her even closer. Her mouth was sucked dry with fear. Fear at what must come next.

'So are you satisfied now?' It bewildered Helen that his voice came out as steady and almost relieved.

'Satisfied. You stupid, stupid boy. I had such hopes for you but...'

Simon's expression remained bland and unreadable giving no clue to the true state of his mind. There was so little Helen knew about him. His next words were spoken with no higher a level of emotion than if he'd been reciting a shopping list. 'Helen and I will go right away to pack and we'll be leaving for Scotland before lunch.'

From a handful of kisses had sprung this? 'Pack? What are you talking about?'

Simon's mouth softened indulgently as he reached out to stroke her hair, 'You didn't think I was going to leave you here did you?' Helen hadn't thought anything.

'Don't worry Alice, I'll be speaking to Paul myself. I'm not a complete louse, I never intended to sneak out. Some husbands might have seen it coming but he's not the most observant person is he?'

Anger was making Alice shake, scaring Helen half to death. That was all she needed to be responsible for killing Paul's mother. 'You're shameless. What are you going to say? "By the way father I've committed adultery with your willing wife and I'm taking her to live with me"? That about sums it up nicely I should think.'

Simon's fingers dug into Helen's palm, his only sign of distress but she made no reaction having the sensation of being a mere observer to the whole conversation never a participant.

'It sounds as if I've missed something.' The usual quiet top layer to Paul's voice was a bare veneer on his patent anger. Helen wondered how much he'd heard but really it was

121

irrelevant because Alice would be only too happy to repeat whatever he'd missed. There might not be etiquette rules about leaving your husband but this public humiliation struck Helen as unwontedly cruel. Nobody should have their life destroyed this way.

'Helen, I'd like to talk to you alone please.' Before Simon could argue his right to join them she agreed. The only thing Helen could give Paul now was the appearance of dignity. Reluctantly she followed Paul to his study where he sat at his desk, as rigid as if carved from marble.

'So, is what I heard Mother say true?' The hair splitting definitions no longer mattered. She'd earned every bad thought he now had of her. 'Yes.' No word had ever been so difficult to say. A brief searing pain broke across the steady glare he had fixed on her but Paul remained upright and disturbingly blank. 'Right. Well I don't think I'm ready for any more details right now. I'd like you both to leave as soon as possible. You'll be hearing from my solicitor.'

Was that it? Ten years of marriage reduced to a curt dismissal. Did she want him to put up a fight for her? If he'd bloodied Simon's nose would she have given in and pleaded forgiveness? That question wasn't going to be answered. Instead she was being treated like a discarded piece of rubbish thrown out of the car window. Helen struggled for something conciliatory to say, anything to make it less brutal but he turned his back to her. On her and everything they'd had.

The train carriage was almost empty. With a seat's width between them Simon wisely made no move to comfort her. Locked in a box of misery tears streamed down Helen's face. She knew without having to be there precisely what Paul was doing right now. Behind the locked door of his study he was lying over the desk crying helplessly as wild thoughts ran around his head about how this had happened. Helen had no doubt of this because it was exactly what she felt. She could make no sense of her weakness. And it was weakness. It had to be. No excuses made this right.

Simon picked up a magazine and flipped casually through the pages. He could wait and would for as long as it took. He'd always been a patient man.

CHAPTER SIXTEEN

*'You don't know why you can't turn around
and say goodbye
All you know is when I'm with you
I make you free
And swim through your veins
like a fish in the sea.'*
Uncle Kracker 'Follow me'

'If I hear one word in the village about this Mother I'll know where it came from. As far as anyone else is concerned Helen is simply away visiting a friend – okay?' His matter-of-factness masked the frustration eating away at him. Helen hadn't wanted to go but the pictures conjured up in his mind by her confession had been too potent for logic.

Alice had never got past treating Paul as a little boy to whom you would explain things slowly and clearly – his being nearly fifty made no difference. 'Think about this carefully dear – your wife has freely admitted to sleeping with your own son. You can't seriously want her back?'

Swiftly crossing the room he thrust his face inches from hers, the veins in his neck bulging. 'Mother, you'd better listen to me,

I love Helen very much and I don't need any more harm done by vicious gossips. You'd better understand that.' He stormed from the room unable to trust himself. It was his father he really dreaded facing, Jack's quiet disapproval had far more power to hurt.

A searing waft of expensive perfume floated his way as Anna stood calmly at the bottom of the stairs, suitcase in hand. Helen's description of the girl's eyes being cold as steel was pretty accurate but something about their unfathomable chill was exciting as they slowly moved over him.

'Paul, could I trouble you for a lift to the station. It seems I've been abandoned.' Some of his initial anger at Helen flooded back. Anna shrewdly read him; he was going to be such a pushover it wouldn't even be funny. This would show that moron Simon how sweet revenge could truly be.

Until this second he'd never been one of those middle-aged men craving a flashy sports car to stroke their egos but a woman like Anna wasn't made to ride in a dull green Volvo, where there would be no flash of her legs sliding into a low-slung seat. Here was the type of woman who might wear stockings outside of the bedroom. Helen had never even worn them inside it.

It was an effort to concentrate on the road.

He hadn't thought to ask when her train left. She knew they were an hour early. Paul's commonsense had departed; the humiliation burning him like acid.

Paul almost demurred at her suggestion of a quick drink in the pub but minutes later was sitting next to her at a dark corner table in the King's Arms; his left leg only a few dangerous inches away from her flagrantly slit black skirt. It was hard to keep his eyes away from the creamy skinned thighs it revealed. Draining her first gin and tonic in a single swallow, Anna leaned back, and smiled slyly waiting for him to fetch another. He only dared to drink orange juice.

While her hand gently massaged his tense shoulder muscles Anna uttered soothing words, praising him as a good husband patently unappreciated by Helen. His bruised ego soaked up the liquid sympathy like a dry sponge.

After another replenished glass her fingers casually unknotted his tie and loosened the top button of his shirt. The blood thumped crazily in his head and everywhere else. 'That's better isn't it?' Her low voice purred like a satisfied cat. Paul was afraid he'd explode like a frustrated teenager right where he sat. He was too afraid to move.

'I can always catch the later train.' Paul was flashed signals he couldn't quite believe. He must be misunderstanding because women simply didn't proposition him. The occasional doting female patient came with the job and the white coat but that wasn't serious.

Later that night when he lay awake crippled by his stupidity Paul couldn't say when he'd agreed – maybe he'd just not disagreed? It might have been when Anna leaned so close his eyes were drawn to the front of her clinging white silk blouse, not quite buttoned up as much as it should have been. Or maybe it was when she swung a room key tantalizingly in front of his confused eyes?

In the old fashioned rose-papered bedroom Anna had immediately taken charge, efficiently producing condoms from her handbag while sparing no explicit details of precisely what she expected him to do to her and what she would do to him in return. Some were things he'd only seen in a Playboy magazine. He'd never heard a woman scream that loud except in childbirth – God knows what the people in the other rooms had thought. Somehow she'd coaxed him into managing it three times in as many hours – something that hadn't happened since he was a very horny eighteen-year-old on holiday in Greece drunk on ouzo with a randy Swedish girl called Ulrika.

At the station she'd airily dismissed his tentative suggestion of meeting again, barely able to hide her amusement. He hadn't known women could use men that way.

Helen shook with the rattling of the train and loneliness. Beside her Simon slept. Paul's hurt uncomprehending eyes kept intruding into her consciousness. Maybe if she pleaded he'd take her back. They'd loved each other for ten years so surely that meant something? There was a stop coming up in a few minutes, she'd get off.

Whatever she planned in her head regarding Simon was concerned never turned out. The ritual seemed to be that she could be completely decided and sure but then it would all disintegrate. It had happened every single time.

He'd stretched himself awake, pulled her so close their bodies almost melted together and whispered convincing words of what their life together would be like. There was no reality left at all.

Later when things were different and she was able to bear remembering a few details streaked across like lightening in the sky. There was the dark foggy Edinburgh station, an old jeep struggling to start after being parked outside too long, tea from a roadside van – hot and sweet and served in a thin plastic cup nearly burning her hands. And always there was Simon.

'We're here, Helen.' His soft voice and the crunch of tyres stopping on rough gravel

128

woke her from a gratefully blurred escape. Here was apparently nowhere near any civilization. Cornwall was remote but never in this utterly desolate way. The ink black quiet around them was broken only by the myriad of stars in the clear sky and a large lake shining a deep glassy green in the moonlight.

Simon's cottage was the only place in sight; sturdily built of dark stone and guarded at the back by rough hills. There were no lights from nearby houses for reassurance. Simon held out his hand – giving her a choice.

The warmth of the small irregularly shaped room enveloped Helen. Somebody had anticipated his return. The generous fire burning in the wood framed fireplace and soft dark red lamps lit the comfortable worn furnishings. Her eyes flickered greedily around, only becoming aware of his scrutiny when glancing back quicker than he expected.

'So what's your verdict?' His arms switched from relaxed and open to protectively crossed, his mouth changing from amused to a serious solid line. It was hard not to squirm; let him see she could be cool too. It didn't come naturally.

'Well let's see. You live alone. Your musical taste is eclectic ranging from jazz to classical. Obviously you read a lot, mostly non-fiction history and gardening. Although you enjoy playing chess you haven't done in a while. Also you like fly fishing and hill walking.' She held her breath.

Simon's cultivated blankness burst into gloriously free laughter exploding a tiny bubble of happiness in Helen, much against her judgment.

'Very good Sherlock. Most of that was straightforward but how did you guess I hadn't played chess recently?' His desire was to be the one difficult to read and finally she'd got one up on him.

'It's obvious my dear Watson, the board and pieces are dusty. Your housekeeper can't be very particular.'

'Well in that case I'd better tell Mother off tomorrow.'

The brief fun fizzled out like a spent firework

'Doesn't she know you're bringing me here?'

Simon couldn't meet her questioning stare. 'Well not exactly.' He'd never looked so awkward. 'She sort of misinterpreted what I said to mean Anna was returning with me and I didn't exactly correct her.'

Helen sank into the nearest chair weighted down with worry.

Curling up beside her Simon stopped any more conversation with warm tea-sweetened kisses. So lost in him Helen forgot thinking. The sliding from sofa to floor was seamless giving her no chance to consider how her body would look to him and then it didn't matter anymore. The months of stamped on longing exploded taking them both by surprise. She hadn't known there was this.

Helen wakened with the glow of sunrise, her back stiff from the hard floor. She rested under the weight of his arm flung across her chest with no desire to move. Sensing her movement he twisted to take her face in his hands, kissing her so deeply it filled every inch. This time the loving was slow, locking him into her soul.

He couldn't believe how this woman with her porcelain pale skin held his heart in her strong hands. There was nothing he could do. He was lost. Whatever happened after today they would remember this but would it be with weeping or smiles? With tightly wrapped bodies burning skin against skin they escaped.

'Simon, are you up yet dear?' There was a loud knocking at the door. Chilly air from the long dampened fire needled its way in making Helen pull the tartan blanket comfortingly around her nakedness as she sat up. Her glance towards the window met a pair of shocked hard blue eyes.

'Mother?'

CHAPTER SEVENTEEN

'The best proof of love is trust.'
Joyce Brothers

Hopping from one leg to the other Simon stumbled into his jeans.

'For God's sake Helen go upstairs and don't come down until I call. She's going to kill me and you won't want to be watching. My mother in a temper isn't a pretty sight.'

As she hastily picked up her clothes Helen almost cracked a smile at the sight of this nearly thirty-year-old man behaving like a naughty child. But then she imagined it being her own mother's eyes she'd met a minute ago and nausea swept through her.

She took refuge in what had to be Simon's room judging by the gardening magazines in an untidy heap on the floor and piles of abandoned clothes. Helen perched on the edge of the bed frozen with shame as the woman's disappointed voice drifted up the stairs. Running some water in the sink she washed as best she could, dragging a comb through her limp, tangled hair. Yesterday's crumpled clothes didn't do much to inspire confidence so the reflection greeting her in the mirror wasn't much of an improvement.

Slow measured footsteps came closer. Her nervous breath released a sigh as Simon's lanky frame filled the doorway. The usual tan of his skin barely masked the pallor underneath and an attempt to smile failed at the tight corners of his mouth. Taking her hands his fingers restlessly manipulated her bones to the point of hurting as he struggled to speak.

'She's gone home.'

'Was she very angry?' Idiotic question.

'Well let's see, how does scathing, furious and let down by me sound?'

Their wanting had caused this. Simon went to stare out the window. Would he prefer to be alone? How was she to know the right thing to do? Asking should be simple but she was out of practice.

'Would you rather I went downstairs for a while?'

He remained with his back to her while she allowed him his silence. Helen was good at being patient.

'Come here.' She could hardly bear the tenderness in his face when he turned. Simon moved her to stand in front of him resting his arms lightly around her shoulders.

'Isn't it beautiful?'

Used to the softer charms of Cornwall the landscape struck Helen as stark and plain.

Apparently endless miles of rolling hills stretched out around the lake in muted shades of brown and green while in the distance sheep clung perilously to the rocky ground.

Simon's hold relaxed as his breathing steadied, the view was having the same effect on him as a walk along the beach accompanied by the sound of the tide always had on her.

'It's different to what I'm used to but it is lovely.'

Gripping her tightly Simon swung her around to face him. 'Oh Helen, stop saying what you think I want to hear. I know you've got into that habit but please don't start it with me.' The frustration in his voice set off tears that Helen couldn't hold back as the pent-up guilt and fears poured out. Simon's arms hugged her shuddering body until it finally stilled.

'How about some breakfast?'

Her thoughts zoomed around shifting from one thing to another. Wondering how Paul was managing with his parents. She hadn't only walked out on him. Of course strictly speaking he'd sent her away – she hadn't exactly chosen to leave although she'd probably made it impossible for him to let her stay.

Simon quietly waited and watched the rotations of her mind. 'Come on. I'll cook. Then we can talk. I expect the food will be so bad it'll be an easy decision.' The words were light but the feeling behind them wasn't. So much stood between them. Following him downstairs Helen sat in a kind of daze – the clatter of pans and smell of bacon frying making no impression on her awareness.

'It's ready.' Simon stood with a loaded plate in each hand by the somehow already laid table. When had he covered it with that cheerful red and white checked cloth? He must have gone out to pick flowers because a blue glazed pot of white daisies stood in the middle, the raindrops on their petals shining in the light. Helen picked up her knife and fork before daring to look down. The sight of the glistening food turned her stomach into somersaults. The tea was the only thing that helped, warming some cold inside place.

'Not hungry?' Simon wiped a crust of bread around his empty plate soaking up the last streaks of runny egg. She dabbed her mouth with the napkin before placing it neatly to one side, folding her hands. This was all pretence. She couldn't keep it up any longer.

'Let's talk now.'

Briefly his eyes turned dark with worry. Then he placed the calm expression on again, the one that covered up whatever his real thoughts. 'How about a walk down by the loch? I don't know about you but I

135

could do with some fresh air.'

Maybe it would be easier, 'If you want.'

Closing the door he firmly took hold of her hand as they set off. It was hard not to notice the vivid blue sky dotted with only a few stray puffs of cloud as the warm air caressed Helen's arms.

Sitting together on some large rocks, Helen resisted copying Simon as he removed his sandals and wriggled his toes into the gently lapping water, but then temptation won. Her squeal as the frigid temperature of the lake stung her skin made him grin boyishly.

'A bit different from the Cornish sea is it?' His voice exploded with laughter.

'Well that's not exactly Mediterranean but it's positively tropical in comparison to this. Surely people don't swim in it?' It was impossible not to return his smile.

'Why do you think Scotsmen have a reputation for being hairy and tough? It's because we're dipped in this at regular intervals by our heartless mothers.'

That ended their fun instantly. The vision of his hurt, angry mother was still too raw.

'Helen, are you still bothered by what you overheard me saying on the phone that day?' His words softly echoed in the air surrounding them. Now he'd given her the opening she didn't know how to ask the question. But she had to. Without it there was no way forward.

'Okay – yes I am. You talk of honesty but I'm still not sure I can trust you. My marriage appears to be wrecked and for all I know you're still playing some kind of joke. I want to hear what you believe is the truth and then I'll have to decide.' Lies were what had put a wedge between her and Paul. They had no place here.

Simon's eyes clouded sadly. Later she could pinpoint that as the moment he had known if he answered her the way she demanded they would be finished. There had been nothing else he could do. Either way he was lost.

'Promise me one thing. Listen all the way to the end without interrupting because if you only hear the first few sentences you'll definitely hate me. After that judge me if that's what you need to do.' He took her silence as agreement.

'Everything you heard was true...' Simon's arm snatched her back to sitting, the urge to run away stronger than her promise. 'It was true when you heard it but it's not true now. I had some warped idea of getting revenge on Paul by seducing you. It was despicable and I can't believe I even considered such a thing. I'm not placing all the blame on Anna but she encouraged me – well you've met her. Then when we met you weren't what I'd expected.'

Helen's simmering fury burst out, 'Is that supposed to make me feel better – to know that at least I wasn't too unappetizing?'

'No it's not. I'm only trying to be honest.'

Hysterical laughter slapped down the brimming tears, 'You don't know the meaning of the word.'

A muscle in his left cheek twitched – the only obvious reaction to her vicious reply. 'I was a jerk, I admit it. When I got to know you and Paul and my grandparents I realized what an awful thing I was doing so I tried to stop it by leaving but the problem was you.'

She ought to walk away but was trapped by the torment in his eyes. 'What do you mean?' Answering her his pain was so abundantly clear Helen craved to comfort him.

'I couldn't damn well forget you could I? I came back here, screwed Anna a few times – I'm not going to say we made love – it wasn't that dignified. All I kept seeing was your face. You wouldn't leave me alone. When I went to bed and when I woke up you were there. Then I heard about Julie and it was the excuse I needed to return. I knew it was the wrong thing to do but...'

Helen's made her voice purposely cold and hard before he broke her. She had to hold onto the small amount of pride she had left. 'I'm not convinced and even if it is true quite frankly I'm not sure I want anything to do with someone with such appalling morals. Remember I've been married for ten years to

138

an honourable man whose single lie to me was told through a misguided sense of love. As far as I can tell the only reason you supposedly stopped your little game is because I wasn't as ugly as you expected. I'm going back to the cottage to get my things together and then I'm leaving. You can either give me a lift to the station or I'll get a taxi. It makes no difference. I'm going home and if Paul won't have me back then I'll live on my own. If he doesn't want anything more to do with me I'll understand – after all I disgust myself.' She had to turn away, unable to face seeing what her words had done to him. He made no move to stop her.

On the platform they both stared grimly ahead, not touching. The blue sky had clouded over to grey promising rain that would only add to the gloom. As the train finally pulled in Helen snatched her suitcase from Simon's hand. There was nothing hidden this time in the way he stared into her eyes now. The fierceness of it shook her badly.

'I love you. Remember that.'

Those might be the last words she ever heard him speak. She knew she wouldn't forget them no matter how hard she tried – and try she would have to.

CHAPTER EIGHTEEN

*'Though no one can go back and make a
brand new start, anyone can start from now
and make a brand new ending.'*
Anonymous

'Oh hell Roger, you can't ask me to do this,
no way.'

Paul pushed the phone against his ear, his
blood thumping. His mother's door was shut
at the moment, he'd checked, but if he dared
raise his voice there would be the immediate
tell tale creak of the hinges. That was reason
enough not to oil them.

Roger's plea for money hung in the air.
Helen would never forgive him if she found
out. When she returned, it had to be when
not if, he wanted no more to hide. That ridiculous stupidity with Anna was bad enough
but this

'Come on Paul. I feel bad about Julie too
but you know what she was like. Always the
tart, teasing and flirting with other men. She
pushed me too far that night that's all, what
was I supposed to do?' Maybe Roger believed
what he was saying but Paul didn't. No way
had Julie been like that. 'What if Helen had

boasted of being with another man?– Of course your sainted wife would never do such a thing.' Paul's remained silent. He dared not confide.

Still forty years of friendship were what they were and both of them had known from the beginning of the conversation what the outcome would be. It had just been a dance of control. One that Roger always won. In both their minds Paul was still that lonely eight-year-old, skinny and scared, bullied by the older boys and an easy target for rescue by Roger always so full of swaggering confidence.

'Exactly how much do you need?'

'Hey mate, you needn't make it sound like torture.' Roger's sounded hurt and disbelieving that his supposed friend wasn't being more generous.

'You fucking murdered your wife, what do you expect?' The last sentence exploded in a furious hiss. By some machinations of his logic Roger appeared to have convinced himself that this mess wasn't his fault.

'All right. All right. Take it easy. Meet me tomorrow about one at the Red Lion.'

He must be unhinged. The old Roger would never have suggested something so patently ridiculous. 'Are you bloody mental? Everyone knows us there, we drink there nearly every week and your picture is still plastered all over the town.' God Paul could

141

see it now. The police called. Humiliation. Being struck off.

'Is it?' The blasted man sounded absurdly pleased with his notoriety. This was in an entirely different league to their childish practical jokes but Roger seemed totally uncomprehending of that.

'Is Mount Columb far enough away for you? There's a pub a couple of streets back from the harbour – The Green Man. It's a filthy old place but conveniently unfriendly. It should suit you perfectly.'

He'd run out of excuses. 'I suppose that'll do but you'll have to wait until Thursday evening. I'm not sure how I'll get away but I'll manage.'

Roger laughed roughly, 'Has the old witch still got her claws in you?' It shamed Paul too much to admit fear of his mother. He made no attempt to answer. They agreed a time but gave up on any more false conversation and hung up.

The lock clicked back into place.

Curling up in the corner of the uncomfortable lumpy seat Helen drifted in and out of a distorted dream filled sleep. As they pulled into Polgarth station she panicked. What could she have been thinking of? There wasn't even a possibility he could want her back. The only thing preventing her staying on the train was having no clue of where else to go. The walk had never seemed so short.

It had only been a couple of days but already an air of benign neglect hung about the house. A thin film of grey dust lay undisturbed on the hall table. Shoes were haphazardly strewn on the floor instead of neatly tidied away in the cupboard. Dirty breakfast dishes sat on the counter while a loaf of bread lay abandoned and drying out on the crumb covered board. She tidied up quietly afraid to make any noise in case Alice or Jack heard. Then she relished the small pleasure of making a cup of coffee again in her favorite mug.

'Helen!'

She held her breath as a confusion fought over Paul's face, already thinner and older than she remembered it being.

'Oh thank goodness you've come home.'

Cautiously he opened his arms out. The familiar comforting mix of Old Spice aftershave and antiseptic rested in Helen's senses as she laid her head on the shoulder of his summer linen jacket – the one she always joked made him look like a cricket umpire. Lifting her mouth to his he kissed her gently and unsurely like a teenager on a first date. His lips tasted a little strange and unfamiliar. Pulling back slightly she searched his deep blue eyes for any signs of hatred but discovered only love and relief.

'I'm sorry. I've been such a fool.' What else

could she say? Let him take it where he will.

'We both have, I should never have told you to go. If I hadn't been a bit of a dinosaur I'm sure this wouldn't have happened. Whatever it takes I'll do it. I want you to know that.'

You wouldn't think she was the one who'd committed adultery. His pleading only exacerbated her guilt. It wasn't right. She needed to be shouted at over her bad behaviour, to be forced to work for forgiveness.

'I thought I heard your voice, so you came crawling back then? I told Jack you would. You know which side your bread's buttered on don't you?' Alice scowled darkly from the doorway. Helen certainly wouldn't get any welcome there. Paul's arm tensed but stayed around her shoulder. It would be the first time in ten years if he stood up for her now.

'Mother, I don't want any more comments like that, thank you very much. Helen has come home and that's exactly where I want her to be. We've got problems to sort out but that needs to be without any interference from you or anyone else.' His fingers dug unconsciously into Helen's flesh but she didn't mind.

'Oh please, you're a bigger fool than I took you for. She's got you well and truly wrapped around her little finger and you can't see it. How on earth could you forgive what she did? You're as weak as your father.' Alice's contempt shivered through them both but Paul remained unwavering. She'd never admired him so much.

'You have your opinion but if you want to continue living under this roof I'll ask you to respect mine also.' Alice snorted in disgust. 'I'm sure Helen will make you both a sandwich and some tea before I take her out to dinner.' The woman's eyes narrowed before fixing a look on Helen that fell somewhere between pure hatred and calculated derision.

'Don't worry about us. I wouldn't want to bother your so-called wife. Go out and show everyone what a fool you are. And if people give you strange looks don't blame me – I'm not the only one who knows what she's been up to.'

They were left alone.

'Well we know where we stand there don't we?' Paul might want to appear unconcerned by his mother's vitriolic outburst but Helen knew otherwise. Inside he had to be as churned up as she was but he'd never admit it. She had to back him and go along with the front he was putting up. It meant they were back to incomplete honesty.

Exactly where they'd been in the first place.

CHAPTER NINETEEN

'Repentance is not so much remorse for what we have done as the fear of the consequences.'
Francois de la Rouchefoucauld – Maxims,
1665

It was a lonely effort but Helen persisted. She knew there was no automatic right to getting a thrown away life back too easily. It was the unlooked for moments that grabbed her heart and twisted it until it bled. Being magically loved, unrestrained laughter, and the deep, warm gold of Simon's eyes – it was all there and wouldn't go away. On Tuesday night she'd made promises that had to be kept. There would be no more chances.

People were watching her all the time. Paul to convince himself of her intentions. Alice to see when she would slip up. Jack with a sort of puzzled bewilderment. Friends in the village smiled to her face but hardly bothered to hide the quick resumption of their real conversations the moment she turned away. Helen didn't know where her ordinary settled person had gone and didn't much like the changeable creature inhabiting her head.

As she mixed up a cake her thoughts

strayed to Paul's odd behaviour at breakfast. In a small gesture of conciliation she'd suggested a walk along the cliffs at Newquay after dinner but he'd claimed to be playing in a darts match. If he didn't want to spend time with her (and who could blame him) couldn't he have saved her pride slightly by coming up with a credible excuse? He'd always been hopeless at darts.

Starting on a beef pie for dinner, Helen's eyes prickled with unshed tears. Pink or cream towels – it shouldn't be that big a deal to chose one or the other but yesterday morning it had seemed monumental. Julie had usually shopped with her and alone it was just too hard. It ran through her mind continually how if she'd done one thing differently, if she'd said that one sentence she'd held back, things could have been different. Then they'd be sitting here together now laughing over a consoling pot of tea.

Then the next stage came flooding in when sorrow was overtaken by a lightening flash of anger over Roger. It was typical that he'd managed to get away with murder the same way he'd got away with everything else over the years. Knowing him he'd had a fat Swiss bank account ready and waiting. Others expressed frustration that the death penalty wasn't available any more but to her that would be far too quick. – Helen wanted him to suffer for fifty years not five minutes.

Lock him in a barred cell papered with pictures of Julie and the children. Let him live every day with the sight of what he'd done.

With a sigh she went back to her life.

In a dimly lit bar two men sit together. From a distance they appear to be strangers forced to share a table with neither wanting much in the way of conversation. The taller greying man nervously fingers his glass, hardly drinking, while the heavily bearded one drains his whisky in one swallow, throws his chair back and walks unevenly to the bar for a replacement. It's plainly not his first of the day. Returning he slams his drink down on the dirty table and stares pointedly at his supposed friend.

'So have you brought the money?'

So Roger wasn't going to waste time with pleasantries, well that was fine with Paul. The sooner he could get away the better. There was nothing left to be companionable about. Paul's skin crawled to see the shocking change in his old friend.

The immaculate suits, hand made shirts and silk ties were replaced by filthy jeans and an old camouflage jacket. Always so scrupulous about his routine of fortnightly haircuts his brash good looks were blurred now with a rough black beard and nearly shoulder length unkempt hair. Once Paul had teased Roger about having manicures – the same nails were dirty and chewed to rags tonight.

'Yes, but don't come ask me for any more.'

'Don't worry I'm not going to spoil your perfect little life. I've got contacts and this'll help me to disappear for good.'

A jukebox pushed heavy thumping music into the smoke filled air. Paul shifted in his seat longing to get out of there. It had taken a mere five minutes of conversation for dislike to grown into revulsion. Roger's thick hands wrapped around the glass made Paul clearly picture them beating Julie and knocking her senseless before leaving her lying in her own blood to die while his children played downstairs.

'I must go.'

Roger smirked nastily. 'Leave then. I'm not stopping you. Run along home to your neat little wife and your tidy home.'

When all was said and done there was an unavoidable sadness at the sight of his old friend's promise dissipated like the wind. Paul almost touched his arm in sympathy but a defensive glare from Roger's almost black eyes stopped him. Deep down Paul understood that. A casual goodbye was the only way Roger could face the ruins of his life. Even if he were never put behind bars he'd be in a prison of his own making where life meant life. There was no more to be said.

Helen observed the weary set of Paul's shoulders as he got out of the car. Meeting another woman surely wouldn't leave him so dejected? Anyway if there was someone else why had he been so desperate to get her back? Her unsettled thoughts swirled around like a whirlpool. Should she question him or pretend it was another ordinary evening? By the time she circled through all this he was already hanging his jacket up in the hall. It was a nice evening so maybe a drink on the patio would help. Not a good idea – too many memories there they weren't ready to face.

'Hello dear, how did the match go?' Casual interest, hopefully that would strike the right note. A few seconds' confusion swelled into the silence as she watched him trying to work out what she was talking about. That was the trouble with lies. You had to remember you'd told them.

'Oh not too bad, only I've got a bit of a headache from all the smoke. If you don't mind I'm going on to bed.' He could be telling the truth, he looked awful.

Helen strived for steady and unruffled. 'That's fine. I'm just going to watch the news so I'll see you later.' He didn't want her with him and she couldn't ask why. Every other night he'd been so attentive, making love even when he'd had a long day and always careful to ask what she'd done that day.

She couldn't think what she'd done to upset him. Simon would be mad if he heard that thought. Her ingrained attitude that things going wrong were always her fault made him more cross than anything. Her hand lingered near the phone. Picking it up she listened to the dial tone for a few tempting moments. Carefully Helen hung up and headed for the bedroom. Being pushed aside wasn't what she'd come back for. Of course what she had come back for was largely a still unanswered question. One minute it was possible to be convinced it was for love of Paul and the honest belief they had a good marriage. Other more numerous minutes filled uncomfortably with the dangerous idea that she'd been too scared to risk another kind of life.

The thin lingering moonlight flung the shadows of Paul's rigid body and open eyes into her line of vision. Lines creased his deep pained face into dark hollows.

'What's wrong darling?'

He sat up, wrapping his arms tightly around his knees obviously desperate to hold himself together. Sliding in next to him Helen pulled him close until his quiet sobs beat against her skin. Finally he looked at her with empty eyes like those of a corpse when the soul has left the body.

'Oh Helen I love you so much, you have no idea, but I've been incredibly stupid.'

His wild frightened face was scaring her. 'Is hurting each other never going to end?' She had to hope so or they were both wasting their time. 'Tell me what's bothering you. Remember we promised to be honest. Would it help if I admitted something first?'

There was no humour in his returning laugh. 'It's not going to matter. You can't have anything to say worse than what I've got to tell you.'

She'd better pick exactly the right thing to say. He was close to breaking. 'Darling, it's not a competition.'

Running shaky hands through his sweat spiked hair Paul began to speak.

CHAPTER TWENTY

'What we do to each other, we do to ourselves.'
Jann Arden

For multiple generations the kitchen walls had soaked up as many stories and tears as they had coats of paint – this was simply another. Helen sunk into the chair, her hands spread motionless in her lap. The blue veins shadowed through her fading tan exposing the fragile bond of skin and blood. Her body didn't even appear to belong to her any more. As the steam rose from the tea mug it blurred her vision or was it more tears? She no longer knew.

Anna. Of all people. Logically she had no right to be so appalled considering how much worse she'd done herself. She tasted the bitterness of how her betrayal had been to Paul. She'd driven him to this. There was no escaping the excruciating details he'd poured out before falling back against the pillow in exhausted relief. She'd refused to listen when he'd tried to admit more. There was only so much she could stand.

All these years of oblivious contentment when companionship and a shared purpose had been more than enough had slipped away. Like myriads of other couples they hadn't questioned anything too deeply and it had worked. Now they were asking too much and the answers were destroying them like woodworm in an aging chair.

Helen stared at the phone while her fingers cautiously played with the numbers. The sudden sharp ring made her jump halfway out of her skin. Picking it up the greeting froze in her throat – stopped by the sound of voices already on the line. It was recognizing the other person apart from Paul that made her blood cease to flow. It only took over-hearing a few minutes of conversation to work out the content of Paul's other attempted confession.

Physical unfaithfulness with Anna paled into nothing compared to this unfaithfulness of the heart. To her it was if he had personally violated Julie's dead body. She had been certain the friendship had ended when Paul stood over the lifeless result of Roger's violence. Helen made no attempt to hang up quietly wanting them both to clearly hear the click on the line.

The clock struck eleven. Her tea was long gone cold. The door hinges creaked so Paul must be standing there. Helen couldn't bring herself to meet his eyes.

'I'm sorry darling.' Darling. How dare he

call her that. That endearment was part of their past.

'Sorry I had to find out?' Wrong approach. It allowed him to go on the defensive.

'I tried to tell you but you wouldn't listen.' Bad move on his part. Putting her in the wrong wasn't going to work for once.

'So that makes it all right does it? You're never wrong are you? Oh shed a few crocodile tears over screwing Anna and everything's supposed to be okay. At least I had the guts to admit I'd made a mistake. Actually maybe it wasn't so crazy after all because Simon definitely saw me as more than a convenient housekeeper.'

Paul moved close enough that she couldn't avoid the disdain filling his eyes. 'Don't flatter yourself dear. You know as well as I do what his motives were so don't try to turn it into some grand love affair. If it was so great you wouldn't have come back and we both know that.'

Helen stood, clutching the edge of the table for support. 'Oh yes, and why was the precious Anna so keen to drag you into bed – apart from the lurid athletics I'd rather not have been forced to hear about?' She'd never spoken to him like this. He probably didn't believe what he was hearing.

'I suppose it wasn't like that with you and Simon?' He almost choked on his son's name.

'If you really want to know the sex was great. Fantastic.'

That last verbal punch sunk Paul like a deflated balloon. Pouring a large glass of whisky minus his usual water he swallowed it in one. When he could bear looking directly at her again his eyes were nothing more than hollow pits in his pale drawn face. His voice resonated with pain, 'Helen, whatever are we doing? I really am sorry about Roger and I know I shouldn't have helped him. But he's in a bad way – he's finished.'

A profound heaviness settled in the pit of her stomach as it crystallized that she didn't even want to find a way back from this. They could talk around it from now until eternity but the truth was she no longer wanted either to forgive or be forgiven.

'What on earth's all the shouting about? Some of us were trying to sleep, not that I expect any consideration around here.' Struggling with her walking sticks Alice glared at them both from the open door. At any other time the sight of her pink rollers covered with a hairnet and the thick white face cream would have given them something to laugh about together later but it wasn't going to happen tonight.

Helen's ten years of built up resentments spilled out. 'I'm sorry we woke you but finally I'm going to do something to please you so maybe you won't mind too much. I'm leaving and I promise this time it's for good. You'll have Paul to yourself again and can control his life like you tried to do ours. I'm sure he won't mind in the least. And if you want to spread nasty stories about me around the village go ahead – I couldn't care less. Label me the wicked whore and Paul the saintly husband. It's fine with me. No doubt you've got a suitable replacement for me planned but let me give you one little warning – don't rely on getting grandchildren from wife number 3 because it wasn't me who refused them in this marriage.'

The anguish on her son's face wasn't enough to dampen Alice's triumphant smile. She moved closer and touched his shoulder proprietarily. Roughly he pushed her arm away. 'Helen darling, please don't be hasty. We can work this out. I know we've hurt each other badly but surely we could see a counsellor or something. Other people overcome worse things than this.' Bully for other people was all she could think. The love she'd once been so sure of was replaced by pity, the recent anger draining away. 'You just don't get it do you? I don't want to try any more. I want a life alone, away from here.'

Alice practically spat her words in Paul's direction. 'Well if you fall for that story you're madder than I thought. You know

157

she's going straight to your own son's bed so let her – they deserve each other. She's made a fool of you and sent my grandson away so why not just say good riddance to them both?'

The muscles in his face and neck were taut and the tension in his breath was clearly audible. 'Mother, go back to your room immediately please. I must talk to Helen alone.' He turned from Alice ready to start again. Wrong. She wasn't staying to hear it. 'No Paul. I'm going upstairs to pack and then I'll be gone. When I've got an address I'll let you know through a lawyer. I'm not discussing this with you any more.'

His face, already pale, changed to a frightening white mask. Grabbing her shoulders he squeezed painfully with his strong capable hands forcing her to be still and in an effort to loosen his grip Helen almost fell. One of his hands reached out winding fingers through her hair in an iron hold jerking her back up. 'You're not going like that. You are going to listen to me.'

She dared not show fear. 'Get your hands off me right now or I'll call the police and tell them about Roger. What do you think the medical association will have to say to that? Ever heard of the words "struck-off"?' His hand swung dangerously close – he was going to hit her and there was nothing she could do.

'You bitch, you wouldn't dare.' He pushed Helen to her knees. Afterwards she'd wonder where the courage, or stupidity, had come from to carry on. Her mouth wouldn't shut up. 'Try me and see. Go on and touch me one more time then you'll find out won't you?'

Alice suddenly spoke. 'What are you talking about? What's Roger got to do with this?'

Shaking like crazy Helen still savoured the minute, the first in all these years when she actually held the upper hand. Paul looked sulky, like a little boy caught stealing apples and forced to apologize. His mother would easily forgive him because she always did but it would be another weapon to use against him on the right occasion. He'd pay for this later.

Paul half-heartedly tried for defiance. 'Roger got in touch last week and I lent him some money. Helen's mad about that.' That's right – make it sound as if there's nothing else wrong. While they faced off Helen slipped quietly away. As the argument continued downstairs she packed the smallest bag possible. Only her oldest clothes went in along with a few toiletries in a simple plastic bag. The miniature silver framed picture of her parents protected in a soft sweater. There was no guilt in taking her chequebook and the money in her purse – she'd earned it one way

159

and another.

Helen hesitated at the door returning to the dressing table and gently easing her engagement and wedding rings off placing them on the small pink glass dish, a thirteenth birthday present from her mother. The pale line on her skin was the only tangible sign of her marriage. It would fade.

CHAPTER TWENTY-ONE

'You are today where your thoughts have brought you; you will be tomorrow where your thoughts take you.'
James Lane Allen

Helen idly studied the dying leaves on the scrawny chestnut tree – the only living thing visible through the dirty windowpane. The damp pavement glistened under the dull orange streetlight outside the door. Thank goodness it was Tuesday and not one of her nights for working at the Blue Anchor. They didn't pay enough for her to be forcibly cheerful this evening.

She ought to get her underwear washed out in the sink and spread on the radiator to dry; that way she could put off spending money at the launderette until probably Friday. Apart from that she supposed the hours would pass trying to watch TV on the ancient black and white set and making a cup of tea when it got to be news time. Then she would attempt to sleep in the sagging narrow bed covered with its ugly shiny green nylon quilt. She wouldn't be successful but...

The evening darkened and closed in

around her as sad slow music cried its way in from the room next door. The elderly man living there routinely shuffled past Helen on the stairs plainly afraid she might demand more than a polite greeting from him. After village life where everyone knew your business, and indeed expected to, there was a terrible alienation from the life going on around her.

Twelve weeks. She'd marked off eighty-four days on the farm implements calendar left by the previous unfortunate tenant. The new interesting life she'd imagined living had narrowed to working in a dress shop by day and as a barmaid three nights a week. Helen had come up flat against the reality of an unprotected life. The relief she'd imagined feeling just wasn't there.

She attempted to treasure the good moments like coming back to her flat and heating up a tin of soup, thankful not to have to cook a proper meal. Last Wednesday morning she'd revelled in getting up late before going on a good long walk, a great improvement on ferrying an ungrateful Alice to and from Mothers' Union. But the moments were few and had to be searched for.

It was hard not to keep wondering how they were coping at home. Jack's bewilderment as she'd struggled to explain why she was leaving was painfully ingrained into memory. The explanation had sounded hollow and selfish. Letting go of caring wasn't in her nature.

It wasn't exactly that she'd intended to stay out of touch but as each day slipped by the idea of contacting Paul became harder. It was possible to convince herself that she hadn't called a solicitor because of a lack of money but not strictly true. Somehow summer had ended and slipped into October while the little nugget of fear over Paul's behaviour still niggled. She would allow herself another month of silence.

The damn music brought the tears back again. Helen had never been the sort of woman to cry at sad films and romantic poems but now it didn't take much at all. It might be the scent of a bunch of cut roses on sale like the ones in her own garden or seeing someone eating the fruit and nut chocolate Paul had always loved. Hunched over on the bed Helen's arms tightly held the rest of her in afraid to let go.

A bad copy of Van Gogh's sunflowers mocked from the wall opposite, illuminated by the bare light bulb swinging from the middle of the ceiling. Occasionally the indulgence of picturing her lovely sitting room at home with its soft green carpet, comfortable overstuffed chairs and carefully placed brass-reading lamps was something she allowed – but only rarely. Generally it was far too painful.

If anybody was to ask her advice on leaving a marriage she'd tell them to think twice, then a third time and if that didn't work try a fourth. Nothing was as you thought it would be. Paul's shrewd observation about her reading too many stupid women's magazines might have some truth in it. How many others had read those carelessly written articles and were lulled into believing it wouldn't be that hard? Exciting jobs and young lovers were supposedly there for the asking if only you had the nerve to go for it.

Unfortunately at thirty-five with no recognizable qualifications, little money and even less confidence it wasn't likely to happen. Prospective employers laughed at her out of date office skills and the plan of completing her garden design course faded along with the arrival of the electric, gas and food bills. Alice had mocked Helen as a dreamer and she'd been right. That was galling.

As for the young lover bit, one look in the mirror would dampen that ridiculous notion. Her skin had a dull greyish tinge from spending too long indoors and haircuts were an unaffordable luxury (her previous smart style now resembled Meg Ryan on an extremely bad day). Jack Robbins had told her at the pub last night to get some decent clothes and cheer up a bit. 'Men want a barmaid who looks a damn sight better than the wives they've left at home, you've got a good pair of tits – for God's sake show 'em off.' That was apparently her only asset as the rest of her was way too thin these days, something Helen never thought she'd say.

Thoughts of Simon deviously sneaked in when she wasn't paying close enough attention but the mental image of his beautifully proportioned hands set her skin on fire and she couldn't handle that. Quickly she covered up with an old blue nightdress. There was no silk these days.

No reassuring church chimes helped her through the night only the strident red digital numbers on a travel alarm clock. Occasionally she carefully went around her comforting kitchen in her mind. The vibrant Italian plates around the walls, the gleaming coffee machine, the solid black Aga keeping its steady warmth winter and summer, a breeze blowing in through the open window and ruffling the yellow checked curtains. Places shouldn't mean so much should they? It wasn't the place though but what it stood for. Memories, contentment, the list went on. If she weren't careful she'd be calling Paul. Stupid. Stupid. It wasn't him Helen wanted so badly but everything that came with their life together.

Drifting was all she was fit for tonight so she might as well give in to it.

Many miles away a man perches on the edge of a cold rock with his head turned towards the black water hoping against hope that when he opens his eyes she'll be there with all the lies and anger forgiven. In the harsh unflinching daytimes he knows it won't happen but here in the star lit darkness it briefly seems possible. He deserves this. He'd done everything she'd accused him of so he has to live with it. Without her.

Another man slumps over a kitchen table steadily pouring out glass after glass of cheap whisky and drinking them quickly down. The normally immaculate counter tops are littered with the remains of discarded meals. A steady rain beats against the windows but he takes no notice seeing only the sad contempt in her face when she left. Why couldn't he have expressed how deeply he loved her instead of resorting to disastrous bullying killing any remaining hope? He resents the pitying looks he receives from other people who apparently know more about his broken life than he does himself. He pours the last inch of amber liquid straight down his throat from the bottle – that way it numbs faster. Maybe then he'll sleep with mercifully dead dreams.

CHAPTER TWENTY-TWO

'Regret for the things we did can be tempered by time; it is regret for the things we did not do that is inconsolable.'
Sydney J Harris, Strictly Personal

'Thanks William. I'm just so relieved to know she's safe and I do appreciate you sharing this with me. Give my love to Merrie and the children. Bye.' Paul dangled the phone from his fingers his brow furrowed with thinking too hard.

He'd gone over and over again in his head who Helen might have contacted before coming up with the idea of his friend William – apart from Roger he was the only solicitor they both knew. But what the devil was Helen doing in Bristol? Surely she couldn't object if he sent a letter. Then again he had time off due and James had been trying to persuade him for weeks to have a break so why not go there in person instead?

James had been spouting a load of nonsense recently. There was nothing wrong with him. Maybe he was drinking a little more than usual but in the circumstances that wasn't surprising and at least he wasn't mixing it with addictive prescription drugs like a lot of other doctors he knew; the occasional Prozac didn't count – you could eat those things like sweets.

Visiting Helen was the only way to end this ridiculous situation. Watching his martyred father struggling to help around the house was getting tiresome. He'd nearly bitten his mother's head off a few days ago when she'd suggested getting a cleaner in. Helen would hate to return and find a stranger messing with her house.

It would be good to get away from the surgery where people seemed to be treating him with an odd wariness he didn't understand – so he'd lost his temper once or twice with some of the incompetent fools – he was a doctor not a saint.

The sooner he went the sooner she'd be back where she belonged. This whole thing was crazy. She loved this place and if she didn't exactly love him he loved enough for them both. He could live with that but not without her.

Cold damp air blew in through the partly cracked car window. Paul had to keep fighting a bone-numbing tiredness. The roads were clear so it shouldn't take long. He'd made a mistake telling James where he was going. That had brought on another lecture about being absolutely sure he was doing the right thing.

His partner was good at his job all right but could be a bit of an old woman. Late 30s and never married which made Paul wonder sometimes. He didn't appear very interested in women so perhaps he was the other way inclined? There had been a lot of that at school and Paul had always thought it a bit unnatural, but these days you couldn't say that. He missed Roger more than he'd dare admit – everyone needed someone they didn't have to watch their words with. Helen had never understood that.

James let the phone ring about twenty times before hanging up. That was the third time he'd tried in the last hour. For some reason he couldn't have articulated he felt uneasy. He wasn't as sure as he'd been a few months ago that Paul wouldn't do anything stupid.

Helen was trying to make up her mind whether or not to go to the cinema with Kim and Callie from the shop. Listening to a couple of twenty-year-olds drooling over the equally juvenile Leonardo di Caprio wasn't exactly her idea of a fun evening but it might be better than another night in. As she dithered heavy rain started to beat on the glass and that decided her. Better the dull warmth of her room. The phone rang annoyingly downstairs but she left it – let someone else answer it if they cared.

Now one of his damn wiper blades had come lose and what was the betting he couldn't find anywhere open this late to fix it. The rain came on harder and Paul's eyes itched painfully. Maybe it would be better to stop for the night and see Helen tomorrow instead; it was getting late to turn up unannounced.

A large white van loomed in front of him with its horn blasting. Squealing the brakes badly he swerved to avoid it and pulled over by the side of the road his hands trembling on the wheel. A couple of whiskies and they'd be steady again. Paul drove cautiously along rows of rain soaked streets until a lighted pub sign showed through the gloom.

This was better. The warm smoky atmosphere along with the strong liquid in his glass bolstered his courage. It was a pity he'd forgotten all about lunch because the thin sandwiches curling up on his plate weren't going to do much to soak up the alcohol but they'd have to do. The bonus to spending the night here was not having to watch the number of drinks he had so it would be easier to achieve oblivion, the only way he'd been able to sleep recently. Then in the morning he could buy Helen flowers before surprising her at work. Problem solved.

Through the haze a pair of long shapely legs dangled tantalizingly from a barstool. They were attached to a not bad-looking blonde in a short red skirt. A bit clichéd with her stiletto heels and overdone make-up but the welcoming smile coming in his direction made that somewhat irrelevant. He had a good excuse to head that way, his glass was empty again. Paul swallowed a Prozac dry first – that would speed up things a bit.

'Can I buy you a drink?' Close up she wasn't as young as he'd thought but what the hell did that matter. Of course she accepted, it'd been a quiet night and a gullible stranger was an unexpected bonus.

'Double gin love, thanks.' No point in messing about. Better get in there quick before someone warned him off. He was well away already so she wouldn't need to do much. Probably he'd pass out as soon as he hit the bed and wouldn't miss a few notes from his wallet either. She knew the type – he wouldn't want to report it and be thought a fool, which he was. Pete the barman would let her use an empty room in exchange for a little reward later – no problem. After a couple more drinks and listening with what she considered was quite well acted interest to Paul's ramblings about his dozy wife Flicka thanked her lucky stars she hadn't ever been stupid enough to marry.

171

Things were fuzzy in Paul's head. He'd meant to keep track of his drinks but some time after number five he'd given up. The woman listened so sweetly to him and her musky scent smelt so enticing when she let him rest against her shoulder. Her kiss surprised him but in a good way, inside he was so desperately lonely.

What was she saying? Something about a room. It would be good to kick his shoes off and lie on a comfortable bed. The stairs were hard to climb and he couldn't work out if that was because they were steeper than usual.

Arrows of bright light pierced his brain. Opening his vision filled with blue flowers moving in violent circles. He slammed his eyes shut again. As Paul rolled over his insides did too. Cold air prickled his bare stomach so he pulled the covers up over his naked body. With great caution he tried looking again and gradually the room slowed to a halt.

Holding his head perfectly still little snippets of memory began to creep back. He could recall being in the bar last night and probably having too much whisky judging by the state of his furry mouth. There had been a woman. She must have lain next to him by the sickly smell of her stale perfume remaining on the pillow. He groaned remembering rolls of soft white soft flesh when she'd released her body from the too-tight clothes, her breasts like unbaked bread dough. How the hell had he responded to that? The only slight consolation was that he didn't think he had done.

How was he going to face Helen like this? A lukewarm shower helped but yesterday's clothes showed up his neglect. He'd have to buy a razor on the way – supposedly fashionable modern stubble only made him look like a derelict. Picking up his comb and keys from the bedside table Paul automatically checked before putting his wallet in his back pocket. The money was gone. Shit. This was a bad start to the day. But it would be all right. He was going to see Helen. She'd make it okay.

CHAPTER TWENTY-THREE

'Whatever needs to be maintained by force is doomed.'
Henry Miller

'Helen dear, there's a Dr. Watkins here to see you if you feel up to it. Only for a few minutes mind.'

As she managed a barely visible nod shards of pain throbbed through her head. Her gaze fixed on the bare tree outside the window stripped to a skeleton by the cold wind. James's worried face came into view as he bent over and kissed her cheek.

'Oh Helen, how are you? I'm so sorry to see you like this. If I'd thought for a minute that Paul was capable of hurting you, you know I'd have tried to stop him.' Helen sunk back against the hard hospital pillows, her face equally as white. Without needing to be asked he held a glass to her mouth with the straw tilted just right so the cold water could relieve her throat, still sore from the newly removed tubes.

There was one question she desperately wanted to ask but Helen had no voice for it. Her agitated fingers plucked at the sheets

174

while a sad darkness lurked behind her weary eyes.

'What's wrong, Helen? If it hurts too much to speak can you manage to write something down?' It would hurt to speak in more ways than it was possible for him to imagine. James placed a pad of paper on a tray in front of her and a stubby pencil gently in her hand. Through incessant pain and giddiness Helen managed one scrawled word. 'Baby.'

Briefly James lowered his head but when he raised it again she read the answer in his soft brown eyes before he spoke. 'I'm sorry. You lost the baby I'm afraid.' Living in the village there'd been no way to avoid hearing the stories. More letters appeared. One name. It wasn't hard to guess what she might mean but James had to be sure. 'Are you telling me Simon was the father of your child?'

He waited until he heard the pencil drop from her fingers before reaching over to read the solitary word, 'Yes'.

'Did Paul know? Is that why...?' He couldn't put into words the question as to whether that was why she'd been beaten unconscious. Helen's head barely moved in acknowledgement, strained exhaustion etched into every pore of her skin.

'Would you like me to contact Simon?' The question made her flinch in a sort of desperate panic. James held her hands, surprised at their bony thinness, and murmured calming reassurances until she relaxed against the bed her eyes closed in utter stillness.

'I won't do anything you don't want. I promise.'

Beneath the bruises she attempted a grateful smile but it trailed off to plain resignation. James left and she was alone again. Truly alone with the hopeful life inside her extinguished. She didn't deserve comfort anyway after what she'd done. What was wrong with her? Why couldn't she have been satisfied? Was satisfied such a terrible thing to be?

Helen had never known before now how slow hospital days were. What did you do when television caused your head to ache more and books were too heavy to hold? Thankfully dear James had arranged a private room for her, as having to cope with the inconsequential chatter of other people would have been beyond unbearable. There were far too many minutes where there was nothing to do but be forced to remember.

It tracked through her brain like a constantly running horror film.

Her day at the shop had lulled with its ordinariness. Strangely it'd been the first time she felt really well in ages. She'd hugged to herself the result of the test she'd done the week before. For a doctor's wife Helen knew she'd been dense. Why hadn't she associated the nausea and swollen breasts with pregnancy? Denial probably. It had been the unthinkable. Only one man could have been the father. Paul was always far too careful for that.

The walk home had been so routine. Stopping at the butcher's to pick up a pork chop to grill for supper, getting a newspaper and some oranges from the shop at the corner of her road and then climbing the three flights of stairs to her flat. Looking back Helen faintly recalled noticing the unlocked door. Securing the windows and doors had always been Paul's job and the habit wasn't reliably ingrained yet so she'd thought nothing of it.

There he'd been – sitting in the only comfortable chair in the room and turning to smile as she entered. It had even been cheering to see his familiar face. Willingly she'd followed his suggestion to turn the key in the door for her own safety. For the first few minutes they'd swapped polite conversation, how they both were and how she was managing. Like two old friends meeting.

Her first niggle of disquiet had come as she'd noticed his unnaturally flushed face and the peculiar flexing of his hands that he seemed unable to stop. Paul had struggled to sit still as his conversation became faster and less coherent. To calm things down she'd offered tea and he'd accepted.

Walking across the room was her big mistake. Fancy forgetting how doctor's surreptitiously studied patient's bodies to add information to what they weren't told. That orange stripy sweater she'd worn because it was chilly had started to cling. That was the moment his face fixed into an awful paralysed mask and a choking sound came from his throat as he jumped up and came towards her until he was only inches away from her face. His breath had been warm and stale. That had been odd as he was always so fussy about personal hygiene. What an inane thing to have noticed.

'You stupid, stupid, slut. That bastard son of mine has got you pregnant hasn't he? About four months I'd guess. When were you going to let me know I'd be a grandfather?'

The force of his hand viciously smashing into her jaw stopped any answer. Somewhere there were screams along with the bitter iron taste of blood in her mouth. Then falling and blankness took her thankfully into oblivion.

The old man in the next flat had saved her – her screams waking him from his musical reverie. Some remnants of long ago army training resided in that seventy-year-old body giving him strength to kick down the door. She wished he hadn't. It would have been better to let Paul finish what he'd started.

The nice policeman sent to interview her hadn't wanted to accept her decision. Through his eyes she saw a vicious man who deserved to be locked up but through her own only a man who'd stood by her side and promised to love and cherish her for life. He'd done exactly that until she'd made it impossible. She would get well and then take care of Paul if he'd let her. It would be her apology.

CHAPTER TWENTY-FOUR

'Nothing can so pierce the soul as the uttermost
sigh of the body.'
George Santayana

'Happy New Year!'

Surely nothing could be worse than the last one so it had to be worth drinking to. Helen unenthusiastically sipped the glass of sparkling apple juice, purposely bought for the occasion. There was no party tonight. Their memories were still like barely healed cuts. Every single day of the last nine months had been endless.

The first time Helen accompanied Paul to an AA meeting and he stood up to admit to being an alcoholic she knew she'd have to stay forever. This was to be the lifetime payment for her selfishness.

Physically she could give the impression of being unchanged, if anything looking outwardly better as guilt and unhappiness kept her thin, unlike Paul who appeared years older, walking with a slight stoop and with no trace of his youthful black hair left. Within days of what they delicately referred to now as 'the accident' it had turned completely white. Occasionally the shadow of a smile would lighten his serious mouth but it went no further. He never dared touch her and there were still too many times when the sight of his hands made her shiver in awful remembrance.

'Happy New Year darling.'

They desperately needed a kindness between them that went beyond duty and the first effort would have to come from her. He dared not make any move. The thought of enduring the rest of their lives without affection was like a slow death sentence. Surviving without sex was one thing, that had only caused trouble anyway, but not without caring. She wanted those four words to start them on the path back.

By February they cautiously shared the occasional joke again and by March a bedroom. One night Helen leaned over to kiss him goodnight but the pulled back restraint in his response saddened her as his body tensed with the effort of not succumbing to the pleasure of contact. The days of uncomplicated lovemaking were gone and it was difficult to believe they'd ever cross the minefield of lies and hurt separating them but she had to keep on hoping – it was all she had.

Spring slipped warmly on into another summer. Like two friends sharing a house it worked most of the time. She sought to make herself grateful for that. As she stood in her beloved kitchen making a cake, a rare occurrence these days, Helen reflected how she'd slipped into a sort of contentment. Between her revived gardening course and some volunteer work she wasn't home much and somewhere along the stony road the spectre of Alice's disapproval had faded. The older woman no longer had the power to frighten her any more. The discovery of some inner strength had achieved what the previous thirty-six years of living had failed to do.

The thing Helen mourned most was her lost friendship with Jack. Adultery went against everything he'd been brought up to believe in so she was not to be forgiven. The toned down version of Paul's violence that he'd been given had horrified him but not enough. Now Jack's aging body was fading daily – that too was part of her self-imposed penance.

How priggish she'd been in her condemnation of Alice and Jack's marriage – of all people who was she to say that what anyone did to survive fifty years together was good or bad? Things were rarely what they appeared to be on the surface and no one could ever really know the deepest workings of other people's hearts.

With a sigh Helen continued mixing and scraping the dry mix from the sides of the bowl. It was all she could do for this one day.

Paul's hand idly stroked and lifted her hair fascinated by its new length. If she'd reacted he would have stopped. They would keep this vigil together as the sun faded and the dusk crept stealthily into the house. It would be over by morning. They sat in the shadowed corner of the room watching Alice's bent head in the remnant of light showing through the drawn curtains. Jack's rough breaths rattled in the quiet air and after each they held their own wondering whether it had been the last, only letting go again when one more was dragged up from his worn-out lungs.

Then there was a silence like none she'd ever experienced. Paul's shell of control broke and he sobbed out his grief. It was Alice who showed unexpected dignity holding her husband's hands until they chilled and stiffened before turning to her son with a simple request to do what was necessary.

'James, please come quickly. I don't know what to do with Paul.'

She tried to keep the panic out of her voice but failed miserably gripped by fright. For the third day in a row Paul lay in their darkened bedroom soaked with a combination of sweat and a bottomless pool of tears. He shook with the effort of not drinking – aching for the escape he believed it would bring. When he did speak all he talked of was how he'd killed his father by his behaviour. Helen tried to share the blame but it did no good. He wasn't hearing her any more. The sight of the full bottle of sleeping tablets he kept by the bed scared her but not enough to make her take them away. She hadn't forgotten.

Alice's voice was steely and determined, 'Oh no, Helen he's not going. Not my son as well.' James insisted it was the only way – a few days in the same clinic as before to get Paul back on his feet for the funeral. Helen knew she was going to sound weary and pleading, which would never be successful, but couldn't stop it. 'Alice, we don't have any choice. He's ill and needs more help than we can give him. Surely you can see that?' Her mother-in-law might know the truth in her heart that but it didn't mean she'd give in.

'I'll agree on one condition...'

'Alice, we both know I don't need your permission, so whether it upsets you or not Paul has to go.' This was deteriorating and Helen didn't know how to stop it.

'Now you listen to me young lady, and remember who this house belongs to.'

Alice delivered her coup de grace. 'If Paul goes I'll call Simon. I need my grandson here.' Helen couldn't believe what she was hearing. Of all things that was the worst she could do.

'Please don't do that. I don't expect you to care about me but don't do this to Paul... You'll destroy him.'

Her persuasion failed.

Paul left peacefully enough with James, unresponsive to her hug, fixing flat empty eyes on her and only briefly reaching out to touch her hair in farewell. As she'd packed a bag for him he'd perched awkwardly on the edge of the bed clutching a photo of himself as a laughing toddler on his father's lap, love beaming from Jack's wide smile.

Alone in their bedroom Helen stripped the sheets and flung open the windows desperate to rid the air of the scent of hopelessness. She had four days to pull everything together. It would never be enough to be able to face Simon again.

CHAPTER TWENTY-FIVE

'Never pretend to a love which you do not actually feel, for love is not ours to command.'
Alan Watts

White lilies again. They would never grow in any garden of hers.

Helen concentrated her attention on steadying Paul's arm as they followed his father's coffin down the aisle. To all outward appearances he was fine, immaculately turned out in his black suit, white shirt and black tie, his shoes polished to a high gloss but this church full of people hadn't seen her dressing him like a little boy. She'd watched from the bathroom door as he shaved himself but had pried the razor out of his hands, as he stood frozen in apparent horror at his reflection. Picking a few stray hairs off his collar her touch set off an involuntary shiver that passed straight through him down to her fingers.

It was her responsibility to get him through this.

The multitude of distractions like refilling

glasses and making more sandwiches when it looked as though they'd run out took her mind away from all the other threatening things. Helen avoided like the plague the corner of the dining room closest to the window where Alice, dressed in the severest of black dresses complete with a heavy, almost Catholic veil, sat exuding an admirable composure. It was broken occasionally by a dab at slightly pink-rimmed eyes with a snowy white lace handkerchief (Helen had been sent to town yesterday specially for a suitable one). Simon was installed in the chair next to her ready to be shown off.

No matter how hard she fought it Helen sensed his presence from wherever she was in the room. The way in which he continually fiddled with the knot of his too-tight tie clearly wasn't caused only by the warm stifling air either. They hadn't spoken. Her only relief came from knowing that Paul was safe upstairs being taken care of by James – he couldn't have taken any more today and certainly not being in this room filled with questions and tension.

Briefly her eyes lingered on the back of Simon's head as he bent over slightly to catch Alice's words. The jet-black shine of his neatly tied back hair couldn't be hidden. Helen hungered to touch it, run it through her fingers as she'd done that night – the one night they'd had. The knowledge pierced her heart like a skillfully inserted needle that their son, and it had been a boy, would surely have looked like him.

If only everyone would hurry up and leave with their speculative conversation. Helen perfunctorily accepted condolences, holding her jaw rigid at the questioning glances thrown her way. It was terribly hard to hide her resentment that all their relatives and so-called friends would love to find out what had gone on these last few months. Probably few believed the concocted story they'd spread about her supposed fall and Paul's stress related illness but there was nothing else to do except keep her head high and her mouth shut.

The sound of crashing glass instantly silenced the chatter.

Helen made her way towards the kitchen desperate to quash the irrational fear sprouting inside her. Something must have got broken. That was all. Pushing past the group of people blocking the door Helen couldn't make sense of what she was seeing. A large jagged hole in the window exposed her garden to unfiltered view. Her eyes flickered quickly over the table. Paul, red-faced and sweaty, stumbled and wove unsteadily around flailing her carving knife wildly in his right hand. It glistened an ominous shiny red in the sunlight. He lunged towards her but it was like watching a film in slow motion that she didn't have a stop button for. James's hand shoved her to one side then pushed Paul roughly to the ground. The second his body hit the floor all the fight left it and he lay still as the dead.

It was the sight of Simon sliding towards the ground with his white shirtsleeves frighteningly dyed a deep crimson, which finally broke through her near hypnotized state. Throwing the tray crashing onto the table Helen flung herself across the room. Barely inches before his head would have crashed she grabbed hold of him, jarring her knees as she slammed into the slate tiles.

Cradling him in her arms she stared into his eyes willing them to stay open. Helen was hardly aware of James pressing on Simon's arms in an attempt to stop the bleeding. She drew closer, enough to hear the words she'd thought never to hear again, the ones that had haunted every waking and sleeping moment since leaving him.

'Oh Helen I love you so much.' In his ear she whispered her returning promise over and over hoping it sunk through his pain. She caught James's penetrating look but could only shrug helplessly.

Helen sipped lukewarm coffee, at least that's what the label on the machine had called it, unnoticing of the people walking busily up and down the hospital corridors. She couldn't avoid the title of betraying wife this time – there were too many witnesses to her abandonment. The moment she got into the ambulance with Simon instead of the car taking Paul back to the clinic that decision was made. The village would buzz with gossip tomorrow and Emily Grant's profits would soar.

Six hours and twenty-seven minutes. This was when she wished not to have the acquired knowledge of a doctor's wife. The promised simple surgery was taking longer than it should. Her mind calculated every possible complication, nothing as simple as a needed instrument or the surgeon taking a break, it had to be a heart attack or a blood transfusion gone wrong.

James slipped into the empty seat beside her and together they watched the hands of the clock creep slowly around. She'd never understood why he made Paul slightly un-easy. Too many people fill the void of worry with inconsequential rambling conversation but he wasn't like that. When finally she needed to break the silence in order to stamp on her tortuous thoughts he humoured her without having to be asked. They discussed in great detail his garden, which she'd helped him start, and the Italian holiday he'd taken last summer. As they'd softly laughed together over his experience watching ricotta cheese being made in a distinctly unsanitary shepherd's hut her smile suddenly faded like a worn out light bulb.

A doctor in blood stained green scrubs stood in front of them. She couldn't bear to meet his eyes with the certainty of what she was afraid they would reveal. He had beautiful straight white teeth – if she could see that was he smiling? James was shaking hands with him. Then the doctor left but why hadn't he spoken to her?

'Helen, did you take that in?' Take what in? A repetitive white noise filled her head. James touched her cheek turning her to face him. 'Simon is fine. There were more cuts than they'd realized and some were pretty deep so that's why it took a little longer than expected, but the good news is there's no nerve damage so he should recover fully. He's in recovery now so they'll let you see him when he's properly awake in about an hour or so. Okay?' Helen flung her arms around his neck making him stagger a little while laughter and tears mixed in her relief.

'Good evening Mrs. Barton. What may I ask are you doing here?'

CHAPTER TWENTY-SIX

'Learn from yesterday, live for today,
hope for tomorrow.'
Anon

The two women loved by Simon faced each other.

His father was left to break the grim silence. Even if she hadn't heard from Simon about the man's army days his upright posture and cropped greying hair shouted ex-military. Mrs. Campbell's scorching bright blue eyes sent streams of hatred in Helen's direction contrasting with her husband's warm smile as he held out his hand.

'I'm Andrew Campbell and you must be Helen. Simon's spoken of you often.'

She had girded herself for dislike and resentment but not this simply offered kindness. It almost broke her thin veneer of control but the man sensed her fragility, just like Simon always did and his words became brisk and matter-of-fact.

'We've spoken to the surgeon and he told us the operation went well. It was a long trip down and my wife was naturally very worried, well we both were so...'

Mrs. Campbell's eyes flashed menacingly, 'Don't you dare make excuses on my behalf. If it wasn't for her disgusting sordid behaviour our son wouldn't be lying seriously injured in a hospital bed and don't you forget it. If you don't make her leave immediately then I'll get whoever is in charge to throw her out.' Andrew Campbell held out his hands in a soothing gesture, clearly used to her volatility and not overly concerned by the threat.

James strolled around the corner then whistling cheerily and carrying two more cups of the infamous coffee. Helen seized on him gratefully.

'Oh there you are James, come and meet Simon's parents.'

Receiving her silent plea for rescue he put the cups down on a nearby table, spilling some, wiped his hands on a clean white handkerchief, and straightened his glasses – giving them all a little extra calming time. Holding his outstretched hand towards Simon's mother his quiet politeness made her remember her manners.

'Pleased to meet you Mrs. Campbell, I'm Dr. James Watkins – Paul's partner. We were all so pleased to hear that Simon will be all right. You must have been terribly concerned.' Helen stifled an admiring grin at the way James turned the conversation about. What could the woman do other than agree?

Her chiselled features softened giving Helen a fleeting glimpse of the ordinary woman behind the fierce shell of a severely frightened mother.

A pretty young nurse cautiously approached them then, her eyes moving uneasily from one to the other in an effort to work out whom she was supposed to be delivering a message to. James swooped to her rescue too.

'Nurse, is young Mr. Campbell ready to see his family now?'

Barely suppressed red curls bounced under her glossy white cap as she nodded. Helen understood the girl's relief only too well – James was definitely doing overtime on his guardian angel role today. A venomous look from Simon's mother froze Helen's step forward. She sensed the light touch of James's hand on her arm and its voiceless advice to wait. From somewhere the courage came to look directly into the woman's fury and be gracious.

'Please go ahead. I'll see him later – he won't need too many people at once.'

The thankful relief on Mr. Campbell's face made her sacrifice worthwhile although it hurt as they disappeared into the room on their right to know just how close Simon was. James gently sat her back down and they drank more of the vile coffee.

'Simon knows you're here.'

'How?'

His mouth twisted into a smile verging precariously on wicked.

'Oh well I just happened to have a word with that sweet little nurse and she passed on a message.' James chuckled happily as Helen couldn't hide her amazement.

'You're a saint, James.' She hesitated. Paul's speculations about James could be right but Helen didn't think so. Anyway all he had to do was to say no. 'Maybe you could take little Miss Redhead out for dinner as a thank you?' There was the smile again. 'It's amazing how much we think along the same lines you know. You don't think she's too young for me?'

It was a little crazy to dabble in match-making when her life was in shreds but some-one deserved to be happy so why shouldn't it be James? 'Not at all, and judging by the looks she's giving you I suspect she won't think so either.'

'Five minutes is all they'll allow tonight Helen, so I'll wait and take you home with me after you've seen him.' Their new friend-ship was an unlooked for bonus in this whole mess. Her mother's often repeated old cliché about every cloud having a silver lining was proving its worth. The only problem with believing that was that other less palatable ones such as reaping what we sow rang a bit too true as well.

Gingerly she pushed the door open. Her heels clicked loudly on the tiles making her long to be wearing something less disturbing.

'Helen?'

Moving closer to the light, already dimmed for the night, her fear dissipated a little. It was paralyzingly hard not to burst into tears of relief, but pain and weakness underlay Simon's faint shadowed smile. He didn't need the added burden of her worry tonight.

'Come here love, so I can see you properly.'

Resting her shaky hands tenderly on his bandaged arms Helen bent close enough to lay her head softly against his cheek before lightly touching her lips to his. The strong response of his firm mouth surprised her and maybe him too judging by the heavy sigh he exhaled. A bustling nurse with the drugs trolley made no dent in their concentration. Her request for Helen to leave was made more kindly than she normally bothered with.

He was alive, which was all that mattered. The tomorrows could deal with what was to come. There were no goodnights or goodbyes because every other time they'd said those words it had meant another destructive parting.

James drove them silently home to St. Within. Burrowed under the soft blankets of his guest bed Helen warily closed her eyes but her consciousness pulsed with harrowing shots of Paul's explosive violence. It was an effort to focus instead on slides of Simon's loving face with his smiling gold tinged eyes and sweeping lashes resting on flushed cheeks. Her breathing slowed and deepened enough to rest. The church clock companionably struck midnight.

CHAPTER TWENTY-SEVEN

'There is always some madness in love. But there is also always some reason in madness.'
Friedrich Nietzsche,
'On Reading and Writing'

Propped up against the cold cup of tea was a stiff piece of white paper covered with James's distinctive script. He was that rarest of people, a doctor with beautiful handwriting. Helen cracked a smile reading his urgings for her to eat breakfast and rest. For once she might actually do what the doctor ordered.

The prickling needles of hot water washed away a lot of guilt along with the dirt. Standing dripping wet and wrapped in an oversized bath towel it occurred to Helen that this wasn't a house with a good selection of women's clothes available – unless James had a lot more active private life than she imagined. Her examination of the contents of his wardrobe put paid to that speculation. No way could she put back on her black funeral dress with its awful memories wrinkled into every crease. One of his baggy white T-shirts worn with a pair of running shorts would do to slip back home. Five minutes and she'd be there and back. It wasn't a problem.

Helen hadn't bargained on the kind of effect walking back through her front door would have. A bitter gorge rose in her throat on seeing her once lovely home defiled. Amongst the stacks of dirty dishes spread out over the counter lay the darkly stained carving knife. Pushed back out of the way in one corner was a pile of towels forever marked with Simon's blood. The room stank of stale milk and anger.

Desperately searching for fresh air she picked her way through the mess and threw open the back door. Smashed remains of the red glass jug Paul had wildly thrown were splattered over the patio stones. Desperately Helen swept them up with her bare hands not having any sensation of pain as they sliced through her skin.

Only then could Helen weep.

She wept for everything irretrievably lost. Her husband, dear kind Jack, the safety of her home and for the carelessly broken shards cradled in her bloodied hands. Remembrances flooded back of her honeymoon and standing with Paul in a back street gift shop in Sorrento choosing a memento to bring back to Cornwall. Nothing could be reclaimed now. She'd tried before and this is what it had led to.

As the tears dried to salt on her cheeks the phone rang but, for once, she let the answering machine take a message. Mrs. Campbell's brusque Scottish accent filled the room. Simon was doing well and had asked to see her this afternoon. End of message.

Automatically she began clearing up, unable to leave her home in this sad state. With the kitchen surfaces scrubbed clean and the window covered with a sheet of plastic she worked her way though the other rooms, removing all physical traces of yesterday's horror. Coolly she made the necessary phone calls – to the glazier, to Fred Truscott cancelling the milk, Mrs. Grant to stop the newspaper, and to the surgery to inform James of her plans for the rest of the day.

The hardest call she left until last. She had to know Paul was being taken care of. As a nurse informed her he was fine but still sedated, Helen sent up a silent prayer of thanks. Talking to him would have been asking too much of either of them.

Three suitcases were already full before she panicked, dumping the contents out all over the bedroom floor. Carrying the burden of her past with her through her clothes was the wrong way to go. Helen threw to one side Paul's favourite blue dress; that would never be worn again. Her old pink dressing gown had been the fashion equivalent of comfort food until Simon's first kiss had exploded its blandness away. That joined the reject pile. Then there was the ubiquitous peach silk nightdress. Its beauty was tainted now. Reduced to one small bag with enough clothes to last a couple of days she was ready. More than ready.

Firmly closing the door Helen turned the key, twisting it a couple of times to make sure it was safely locked. Her fingers lingered on the glossy black paint; three layers she'd diligently applied last summer and still looking good, while whispering her goodbyes. The flowers lining the path had drooped and turned brown in the unusual heat but she turned her back on them.

Alice watched openly from the Rectory window. There was no need to hide her interest today. That wicked woman was gone at last. It had taken longer than expected but finally she'd succeeded. Her part in Helen's disgrace had been discreet, or so she truly believed, with a carefully placed word here and there and a couple of strategic phone calls. Hadn't that Mrs. Campbell been surprised at the anonymous message about who her precious son had staying under his roof?

Someone had to uphold standards.

Thinking about her own son wasn't easy. Maybe he'd always been unstable but that wasn't a pleasant idea – naturally nobody on her side of the family ever had those sorts of problems. When he recovered, which he of course would, he'd thank her. There was no reason why he couldn't go back to work – Simon would never file charges – she'd make sure of that. Then she'd move back to live with him and get a housekeeper to take care of them both.

Given a little time it might even be possible to do better than that. Alice had been thinking a lot these last few months and had run through the list of suitable women of her acquaintance. After much consideration she'd decided on the best one – Betty Walden's daughter Marion. She was about ten years younger than Paul. Modest, respectably dressed, widowed young with no children. Absolutely ideal. The girl's father had been a doctor so she'd understand the demands. This would have to be very cleverly done with no mistakes this time.

'Now Dr. Barton it's time for your medicine and then Dr. Williams is coming along to have a chat about how you're doing.'

Paul collapsed weakly back against the pillows only barely alert enough to know he wasn't capable of doing anything as crazy as getting up and walking out of here. Here was the spare white room he'd woken up in this morning. The nurse sitting patiently at the end of his bed reading a magazine had explained very clearly that it was Thursday. Try as he might to get things in order his brain didn't appear to be working properly because Wednesday was nothing but a blank.

Now Tuesday was clear – up to a point anyway. Following his father's coffin down the aisle. Being in the safety of his own bedroom. James going downstairs to get them some food. His own hand retrieving the full bottle of whisky carefully hidden in the bottom of the wardrobe. The too glorious sensation of the heathery liquid warming his blood as it slid down. He'd gone to the kitchen. Had he been searching for Helen? This was when it all dissolved into a mass of red and somewhere in the red was Simon's face. There was screaming but Paul couldn't work out why but he got the very definite feeling of not wanting to know. Discovering might plunge him back into the dark hole he was struggling to claw out of.

Helen. Saying her name ignited a gnawing hunger in the very depths of him. Everything would be all right when they were together again. She would save him from this.

CHAPTER TWENTY-EIGHT

*'Come live with me, and be my love, And we
will some new pleasures prove of golden sands,
and crystal brooks,
With silken lines, and silver hooks.'*
John Donne, 'The Bait'

Helen entered the room to the sound of
Simon and his mother snapping at each
other.

'Mother, please stop it. Why don't you and
Dad have a break and go for some lunch?'

Mrs. Campbell's anger was barely con-
tained under tightened lips but Helen turned
away from it and instead gave Andrew
Campbell an encouraging smile. 'There's a
nice pub about a five minute walk down the
road if you want a change from hospital
food.' Even while he was thanking her and
steering his wife firmly towards the door
Mrs. Campbell still managed to have the last
word. 'We won't be long Simon, the volun-
teers do a perfectly good sandwich, that will
do us for now.'

It was a shy and uncertain Helen who
raised her eyes to meet his. Once she did it
was hard to drag them away again. Simon

looked good – extremely good in fact, increasing her hesitance. He'd replaced yesterday's blue hospital gown with the grey T-shirt and grey sweatpants he usually slept in and lay quite relaxed on top of the covers. Helen received one of those lazy smiles that crept up and snared her heart every time.

'Come here, I'm not going to bite – not until I'm out of here and get you alone anyway.'

His gentle laugh rumbled on wickedly as an unbecoming blush rose up her neck and face. Helen's mixed-up emotions were too close to the surface for teasing and hot tears streamed from her eyes while everything she wanted to say tumbled around her head like a shaken jar of sweets.

'Oh sweetheart, it's okay come here.' Moving slightly he slid her next to him on the bed hugging her as closely as his bandages allowed while they kissed endlessly in the way of back seat teenagers. Their hips touched and every inch in between making the heat grow. Simon groaned and shifted away. Now it was his turn to blush, something she hadn't ever thought to see. 'Sorry darling, didn't realize I was quite that well already.' Picking up the fingers of her right hand Simon stroked them tenderly slowing the blood coursing through her.

A fearful shadow crossed his face. 'Where do I start again with you, Helen? I'm so afraid if I say the wrong thing you'll send me away again.' That thought darkened his eyes to the colour of warm syrup as he took both her hands in his. Was she trembling or was he? She couldn't be sure.

'We won't have long to talk I'm afraid as Mother's bound to be back soon to protect me from your wicked self.' Simon rubbed his thumbs over her wrists massaging in his words. 'I love you. I have to trust you're certain of that by now. Come back to Scotland with me tomorrow and live with me there. As soon as you're free I want us to marry and have a family together.' His hands moved to her stomach seeing the knowledge of what could be. Helen gasped at his touch and her heart twisted in agony – in all that had happened she'd almost forgotten that he didn't know. She couldn't let any more time go by without telling him.

'There's something I should have told you before but...'

Simon's words held a touch of sadness, 'Helen surely you know nothing you say will stop me loving you. Nothing.'

How to start to explain? In her own way she'd managed to arrive at some forgiving place over the baby but... Unconsciously she rested her hands protectively as she had the night Paul had come for her. She would have done anything then to save their child but hadn't been able to do enough. The words eked painfully out and as they did Simon's eyes flashed dark as midnight, sadder than anything she'd ever seen. It was the worst thing she'd had to do.

'The bastard, the dirty bastard.' Tears poured unchecked down Simon's bruised face. It was her turn to comfort today. Holding him tightly the grief of loss drew them together.

'For goodness sake get your hands off him. He's still a sick man thanks to you.'

Helen's instinct to jump up was stilled by Simon's firm hold keeping her close. Then he spoke the same way to his mother as the day he'd silenced Alice's tongue.

'Mother don't speak like that to Helen please or it'll be a long time before we'll talk again. We need to get some things straight. Helen and I love each other and we'll be married when it's possible but until then she'll be living with me at Montrace. Helen's happiness is paramount to me and I need you to understand that.'

Helen watched a gamut of emotions from loathing to love cross Mrs. Campbell's face. She longed to reassure the woman but wasn't sure how. How do you convey good intentions? After all she was only a mother trying to protect her child – exactly as Helen had tried to do.

Simon's next words were softer. 'I'm sorry

to be that blunt Mother, but I really need it to be clear. One day we'll share the whole story with you both, but it's too difficult right now.' His eyes closed briefly with a confusion of different pains.

Putting things off wasn't the answer. Helen instinctively knew that. She couldn't live close to his family unless they knew the complete truth but she wasn't sure she could bear speaking it. Her eyes searched for Simon's approval but found only questions in them. It was time for her to be courageous. 'I'd rather get it out in the open now.' Helen couldn't be sure if the brief glimpse of admiration in his mother's face was real or in her wishful imagination.

With that she began but with a strange sense of removal as if it was someone else's life, maybe even a fictional character in a soap opera. Helen made no attempt to gloss over her bad behaviour – they'd gone past that kind of pretence. Mrs. Campbell's face remained severe until Helen's composure broke at the mention of their lost baby. Then her face softened in shared pain and for a minute she had no words.

Andrew Campbell touched his son's shoulder. 'I'm so sorry.' Simon rested his head on the shoulder of his father's old tweed jacket allowing his hair to be smoothed like a fretful child. A tired pallor showed through his gardener's tan and Helen wondered if she should have kept silent until he was stronger.

Her hand flinched as the other woman's firm unmanicured fingers rested on hers. 'I really am very sorry about the baby. I do understand how hard that is...'

There was a struggle going on behind Margaret Campbell's tear-brightened eyes. All she'd done was love Simon with a mother's love – there should be no guilt in that. Helen needed her to know she understood. 'Thank you. I honestly never set out to hurt anybody.' The brief nod of acknowledgement she received was satisfaction enough.

The comfortable quiet was too precious for any of them to break. That was left up to the nurse bustling in checking her watch. 'Visiting time is up. Mr. Campbell needs his rest or he won't be going anywhere tomorrow.'

'Oh Sally, don't pretend to be such a tough old thing – give us a few more minutes please.' It was amusing to see Simon's charm working so effortlessly on the plain middle-aged nurse as she giggled like a young girl. 'Just five minutes, you naughty man.' There was a distinct flirty sway to her retreating uniform.

Margaret Campbell came close to openly smiling then. 'I ought to warn you Helen, he's absolutely incorrigible. We spoiled him as a baby and then his sister came along who thinks Simon is only one step down from God so this is the result.'

For a few treasured seconds they were an ordinary pair of happily indulgent women. It gave Helen something to hold onto. As it happened they both turned to face Simon catching a big satisfied grin on his tired face.

'Dad take these women away and sort them out and please be here early in the morning so I can get out of this overheated greenhouse and back to some proper fresh air.' Helen stood to leave but Simon's hand held her back. His father spoke as kindly as ever. 'We'll meet you outside, Helen.' Simon hugged him and then kissed his mother gratefully. Helen sensed the wistfulness as Margaret reached to touch her son's cheek.

Helen sank on the bed wishing she could close her eyes and fall asleep next to Simon's warm body. He stroked her hair tenderly and whispered magic words in her ear.

'Tomorrow. Our life will start tomorrow.'

CHAPTER TWENTY-NINE

'The face is the mirror of the mind, and eyes
without speaking confess
the secrets of the heart.'
Saint Jerome 374 AD – 419 AD

They form an unbroken silhouette on the rock. In the chill October air the lightest touch of a kiss warms the back of Helen's bare neck. As the sky drifts from pale pink to flaming red the sun finally rests behind the mountains leaving the lake pooled black as ink.

'Helen.' His voice echoes loudly in the stillness. 'I don't want to rush you but...' Facing him she stares hard into Simon's deep golden eyes – even the colour of night can't dull their glow.

'Come on say it. What did we promise? No secrets. Not any more.' She had never known a smile could tickle in the dark but his did.

'Maybe I should be more patient and allow you to come to it in your own time but I've got to ask if you've made any decision about starting divorce proceedings?' They'd cautiously skirted around the subject for the last few months but he deserved better.

She'd deliberately pushed to the back of her mind his battle with the vagueness of their future.

'You've every right to an answer. I promised you honesty too. I will make up my mind soon – I only wish it could happen without hurting Paul and I know it can't; but knowing and accepting aren't quite the same thing are they?' Her voice sunk to a husky tear-filled whisper, 'How are we going to live with ourselves darling?' He pulled her shivering body closer unable to give any other reply to an unanswerable question.

Sometimes their hearts almost burst from loving so much. It was what made everything else survivable.

'You aren't kidding are you, James?'

Helen's stomach churned with a mixture of elation and unexpected hurt. It was the last thing she'd expected. While she'd been struggling to come to a decision here was Paul taking it out of her hands by announcing his intention to marry Marion Walden. Helen only remembered her as a rather dreary seeming woman, usually seen around the village with her elderly parents. Even the distance of several hundred miles failed to disguise Alice's influence. It was an effort to make her reply come across as calm and pleased. 'A quick divorce is fine with me too. Please wish them both well from me.'

James was as polite as ever but didn't linger on the phone. Helen couldn't blame him - she'd made her choice and he still had to work with Paul. Their brief closeness had almost been too swift to recognize as the good friendship it had had the potential to be.

At five o'clock she stood watching at the window like an old-fashioned wife. Finally his truck tyres crunched on the gravel but his walking of the few steps in to the house took longer than usual. Did he really have to stop and check on the new plants he'd put in by the door tonight? Flinging her arms around him she hugged him so tightly the breath nearly left her. Helen's eyes met the brief surprise in his but then his body willingly responded against hers, postponing talk.

Abandoned clothes trailed like a running stream up the stairs in their haste to match skin with skin. Helen absorbed his warm earthy smell, taking him into her with utter abandonment. There was no holding back. There never was these days. Little things slipped into mind, remembering Paul's anxious questioning after lovemaking to discover if it had been good for her – Simon had no need for that because he always knew. Her whole self came to life, every time she thought it couldn't possibly get better but the more they discovered of the other the more it did. They drifted contentedly off to sleep wrapped like spoons.

Helen woke to the intoxicating stroke of his fingers along the curves of her back and then he became part of her again. The wonderful romance of the moment was interrupted by Simon's rumbling stomach reducing them both to helpless giggles.

'Okay I get the hint. I'll get dinner ready while you shower.'

'Why would I need to do that? I got the distinct impression the erotic essence of manure and mud was a turn on for you? If this has been your idea of complaining I'll take more of the same please.' He lay back with his arms flung up in abject surrender, his face creased with a broad smile.

'Well at the time it was uh – interesting – but now it's verging on smelly.' For her cheek Simon tickled her unmercifully until she was reduced to laughing pleas to stop. Throwing on some clothes Helen escaped, hoarding up in her head the gorgeous sight of him sprawled naked over the crumpled sheets.

With bread warming in the oven and beef goulash simmering away Helen opened a bottle of red wine and poured two glasses out ready. It didn't take him long and soon he ran down the stairs and pulled her into his arms bathing her in kisses. Helen inhaled the scent of fresh soap on his skin and touched the silky newly washed hair, loose around his shoulders. It was close to impossible to turn her concentration back to food.

After three bowls of soup and a plate full of thickly buttered bread Simon sat back in his chair. Sipping his wine he observed her with shivering intimacy. 'Okay, now it's time to tell me what's bothering you.' She didn't insult him by asking what he meant. They both knew she had something to share. Her wariness stemmed from the unformed nature of her own thoughts; of his reaction she had no doubt. Twirling the stem of the glass around her fingers she took another big swallow. Paul would have been urging her to hurry up but nothing in Simon's calm demeanour hinted at impatience.

Slowly the words emerged of their own volition describing James's phone call. In reciting them it shone through like a beacon in the dark that she would be free, and this man watching her so lovingly across the table would be her life. By the time Helen fell silent a huge smile wreathed her face setting her quiet beauty on fire. Simon's right hand confidently touched her chin as his glance bored into the depths of her glistening eyes. He spoke only one word but it said everything for them both, 'Good.'

Although it's late in the afternoon he sits

215

hunched over on the bed, still in his pyjamas, drumming agitated fingers on the table and ignoring the pot of freshly made tea. If his mind would only clear perhaps he wouldn't see Helen's face every time his eyes opened. The grandfather clock on the landing outside his door strikes four, meaning Marion will be here soon to take him home. Only it isn't home without Helen. This isn't going to be any good.

The old Paul would never have lied, he'd been an honourable man, but these days it slips out almost automatically. There are lies to the counsellors, to James and most of all to the innocent Marion dragged like an innocent fly into his mother's web of control. Imagining Helen and Simon happily together causes a pain so physically acute he swears it's real. The old rational doctor he'd been would have scoffed at the ridiculous idea of anyone dying of a broken heart. Not any more. It would be preferable to this version of living hell.

Sighing miserably he drags himself to his feet and begins to dress. Knotting his tie carefully and smoothing down his hair Paul packs the last few things in his bag. On the top goes his copy of the papers setting into motion the divorce he doesn't want. Now he must start the biggest act of his life and hope he can survive it.

CHAPTER THIRTY

'As memory may be a paradise from which we cannot be driven, it may also be a hell from which we cannot escape.'
John Lancaster Spaldings,
Aphorisms and Reflections

'Are you sure it's not too soon Paul?'

James noted the barely perceptible trembling when he briefly lifted his hand from the table, the slight tic at the corner of one eye, and the occasional searching for words. If this was the best his partner could do in disguising his true emotions, and it was something they both knew how to do and recognize in others, he sensed Paul was still in deep trouble.

Dragging a faint smile across his face Paul was desperate to be convincing in his plea to return to work. If he could only keep busy with patients it would save his sanity – it had to. He'd tired of AA meetings, all that exposing your supposed weakness to a bunch of losers. It wasn't hard to do by yourself with a little self-control. He could regulate himself easily, a small sherry before dinner, maybe a glass or two of wine with the meal and perhaps occasionally a watered-down whisky as a treat before bed.

There was one strike against him already. James had caught him in tears yesterday when the post arrived; the sight of the decree nisi had shaken him with its reality written down in black and white. Six short weeks was the only time left before it became final.

Meanwhile his mother continued to encourage Marion with wedding plans. Did they really think he was going to marry that dull woman? When he'd been in the clinic and horribly depressed the idea had sounded appealingly peaceful and safe but back at home surrounded by Helen's things, it was reduced to nothing more than a horrific betrayal. The idea of trading seductive memories of Helen for a lifetime reality of nights with Marion revolted him. She was a good, decent woman and some part of him was aware how unfair he was being to her but love isn't fair.

'Well all right, Paul. We'll give it a try and see how it goes.' Paul almost laughed aloud and said how big-hearted it was of James but sarcasm wasn't a wise move. That was step one achieved. Next on the agenda would be placating his mother and Marion long enough for his plan of winning Helen back. It would take all his ingenuity but he had to do it. Life without her was only bare existence – she had to see that. Simon had to be blotted right out of his mind. Paul didn't dare given any consideration to what this might do to him.

Springtime in Scotland came late. Used to the soft Cornish weather and February swathes of daffodils it came as a shock when even snowdrops didn't brave exposure until well into March. The mornings still began with a carpet of thick white frost and today the sky filled with threatening dark clouds.

None of that bothered Helen curled happily in front of a warming fire, her eyes drooping with tiredness. The fine red wool blanket Simon had bought her last week settled pleasantly around her growing curves. His face when she'd tentatively announced the positive pregnancy test had been worth every scrap of the unpleasantness and guilt they'd endured. It was so different this time.

She'd sat rigid with worry hoping Simon's mother wouldn't be too unkind when he'd phoned to tell her the news. Living together was bad enough but there was no hiding a pregnancy without a wedding in sight. But the smile hadn't left either his face or his voice. Babies were Margaret Campbell's weak spot. There were lots of extra visits these days bringing a supposedly spare pie or cake from her kitchen to save Helen from cooking. The local shops had a lot of bargain baby clothes at the moment that were apparently too good to be left there.

Helen wished she hadn't snapped at Simon last night for suggesting they book a date for their wedding. The theory of being free in three weeks was one thing but who knew? She'd done enough tempting of fate to last a lifetime recently.

Paul glanced nervously at the stiffly wrapped bouquet of red roses, a typical garage forecourt offering, on the seat beside him; perhaps taking indifferent flowers to a keen gardener was a bad plan? Anxiously he smoothed the hair back from his forehead and rubbed a hand over his chin – maybe he should shave again before arriving? His mobile phone was turned off after the six attempts by James to call. It had been damn stupid to confide in him.

There went another of those dizzy whirls in his head again. Eating lunch would be a good idea but his churning stomach couldn't stand the thought. He drained the can of Coke getting a burst of caffeine-fuelled energy, a whisky would steady his nerves better but he mustn't turn up smelling of booze. A couple of tranquilizers would help calm him down. The label said to take one but that was only a precaution so Paul quickly swallowed two to make sure.

He had to wonder where Helen had ended

up as the car bumped roughly down the unpaved track. Why on earth would she want to swap their lovely house in Cornwall for this god-forsaken spot? He supposed the scenery was striking but it was too wild for his taste. Stopping the car he slumped over the steering wheel, swamped by an instant tiredness that came from out of nowhere.

Waking to what felt like grit in his eyes and some kind of dreadful pounding noise in his head Paul wanted to sleep forever. Gradually he focused enough to realize the car was being rocked with torrential rain. Mechanics weren't exactly his forte – proved when he stupidly flooded the engine by trying too many times to restart it. It couldn't be far from here so he'd walk. Not a problem. Logic had seeped from his brain by this time.

After battling through shards of icy water, that's what they resembled piercing his body anyway, lights faintly gleamed from a small cottage barely visible ahead. Ineffectually Paul tried to tidy himself but it was hopeless. Banging on the door with his fist he had no concept what a frightening sight he presented to Helen, with rain gushing down a hollowed face centered with staring white-rimmed eyes.

With her heart thumping in terror her hands reached protectively around her stomach. This couldn't be happening again. Why, today of all days, did Simon have to be miles away visiting a customer? Andrew Campbell would come but would take at least ten minutes and who knew if she had that long. Paul shouted and pleaded to be let in. Her hand moved to lift the latch and he pushed it from her hold falling to his knees and scattering wet crushed flowers all over the tiled floor.

In the few seconds that were all she might have Helen grabbed the phone and dialled quickly, afraid that her shaking fingers wouldn't hit the right numbers. All she got was the chance to say hello before Paul wrenched the set from her hand and slammed it down digging his fingers into her arms and swinging her around to face him.

With one wild flash the lights went out and she screamed, at least there was a horrible sound that Helen could only assume came from her own throat. A jagged blue streak of lightening threw Paul's rigid face into harsh relief. When he spoke his voice was eerily normal but she knew it wasn't to be trusted.

'Sorry about arriving like this dear. Could we sit down and have a chat?' Anybody would think this was an ordinary social visit. Too petrified to admit the truth of her fear Helen moved quietly, setting a couple of thick yellow candles on the table. The concentrated light they shed emphasized her isolation. Somehow she had to keep him at a distance and not annoyed until Simon returned – probably not for at least another hour – what on earth could she do until then?

'Would you like some tea?' God she was turning into her mother with the eternal remedy for any problem. 'We've got a gas stove thank goodness.' The word 'we' made him grimace – she had to be more careful. He followed her to the kitchen, his eyes flitting everywhere and landing on Simon's spare pair of Wellingtons, abandoned by the back door. Everything had too many implications and possibilities for misunderstanding.

Helen carried the tray back into the other room, sitting the other end of the sofa from Paul, and then watched as he noisily gulped his tea making no protest when she leaned over to pour him a refill. After three cups and most of a plate of shortbread his earlier ferocious look was replaced by sheer exhaustion. A small pull of sympathy tugged at Helen. One she didn't want to feel.

'Haven't you eaten in a while?' He mumbled a reply; unable to meet the concern he knew would be in her eyes. 'I'm not really sure, I think it might have been yesterday.' She clamped her mouth shut on the question she almost asked as to whether he wanted to lie down – there was too much possibility for misinterpretation there.

Flickering candles always played tricks with

the light but it bothered her that his eyes, the honest dark blue eyes that had for years gazed at her so openly, weren't focusing properly. She'd often heard him describe that sort of vacant look as a side effect of many drugs. Helen would have to be very careful. She wasn't going to fail this baby too. When finally he was able to look at her again she physically shook with the remembrance of love, a love that had been so much a part of them both, now twisted into something awful and unrecognizable. The hands that once stroked her with desire he had turned into instruments of hate. She could never forget that.

From the corner of one eye Helen watched the slow ticking of the clock while distantly instigating a rambling conversation about the weather, how his mother was, and polite enquiries about old friends in the village. This must be what it was like to tiptoe through a minefield waiting for the maiming explosion to hit. Suddenly he grabbed one of her wrists hard enough to send a jolt of pain through the bones.

'Be quiet Helen.'

CHAPTER THIRTY-ONE

*'If you love somebody, let them go. If they
return, they were always yours. If they don't,
they never were.'*
Anon

There was no single cell of doubt in Simon's
mind after his father's call as to who was in
the cottage with Helen. His Jeep tyres
squealed angrily at being turned too hard
into the corner. Thank heaven he knew the
route well enough to drive it blindfolded
because that about summed up the view
through the rain lashed windshield.

Having concealed his car a safe distance
from the cottage Andrew Campbell crept
along the path never making a sound. Jungle
training wasn't something a person forgot.
He'd pay for this later, as defying Margaret
wasn't something to be done lightly but
there had been no choice. Helen had merely
managed to say the single word 'hello' but it
had so resonated with panic something had
to be very wrong. After more than forty years
surely Margaret hadn't seriously thought
he'd remain sat at his desk paying the

month's bills when poor Helen might be in danger? She'd thought he was overreacting while he only hoped he was.

The rain sodden light was barely enough to make out in the shadows Helen's white face and the shape of a tall man holding her thin wrist tightly. Andrew placed his hand firmly on the doorknob.

'What the devil are you doing Dad? I told you to stay at home. I'll deal with this.'

Andrew Campbell's usually kind blue eyes turned dark and hard as flint in his anger, 'Don't you dare talk to me like that. You've never dealt with anything more dangerous than a garden fork, but don't you ever forget I spent 20 years in the army. I've seen and done things worse than you can ever imagine, so don't even consider telling me I'm not still capable of hurting some soft doctor if necessary.' The ferociousness shook Simon's perception of his father as a gentle, quiet man – the warrior apparently only hidden a shallow layer from the surface.

The apologetic smile Simon gave squeezed almost forgotten memories from Andrew's heart. It had been a while since he'd thought about the day they'd collected Simon from the children's home but now it proved surprisingly easy to recall. The tiny baby lying so lightly in his arms had looked up with those solemn golden eyes wrapping firmly around his new father's soul.

'You know I didn't mean it that way Dad, it's just I'm not a big fan of having Mother's wrath descend on me which will most definitely happen if you get hurt.'

Andrew couldn't blame the boy on that score. Years ago he'd made the stupid mistake of believing her to be a sweet compliant girl until their first argument proved him very wrong indeed.

Margaret's smart red Volkswagen emerged suddenly through the persistent rain and ground to an abrupt stop on the gravel having demolished a puddle foolish enough to get in her way and splashing them in the process. Slamming the door shut her vivid blue eyes swivelled around to land on them. 'Why in heaven's sake are you two standing there like a pair of dummies?'

The men looked at each other – earlier she'd urged caution and now she was berating them for inaction and women didn't get why men found them damned near impossible to understand? 'Well we...' Neither finished the sentence. It was bound to be wrong.

With no intention of bothering to wait for a reply she rapped sharply on the door twice then flung it open. 'Helen my dear, I hope I'm not late. Did you say three or half-past for tea? Oh excuse me, I didn't know you had a visitor.' Her determined body disappeared into the room. All they could do was follow.

'Right my dear, why don't you go and put the kettle on? I think we could all do with a good strong cup of tea. Andrew, you phone that nice Doctor Watkins. Simon, you stay here with me.' Everyone did exactly what they were told. Paul's panic had surged at the sight of them all, visibly shaking and looking like an animal caught in a trap, but then he broke, crumpling to the sofa. The room filled with his loud tears.

Margaret's hands deftly lay Paul down tucking a couple of soft cushions under his head before covering his shivering body with the same warm plaid blanket once used by Helen and Simon – thankfully he didn't know its history. Within seconds his eyes closed in exhausted relief leaving everyone to creep quietly around like parents with a newborn baby, relishing the transient moments when it finally sleeps.

Before daring to come back into the room Helen watched cautiously from the kitchen door totally unnerved to see this man whom she'd once considered an emotional rock and her infallible support reduced to such pitiful emptiness. Had they done this to him or was it always present only waiting for the right moment to be tested? If there was such a thing as the truth she wasn't sure she could handle it just yet and maybe she never would.

With the tray quietly placed on the coffee table Simon made room for her to join him in one of the big comfy chairs. The warmth from the hot drink soothed Helen enough that she couldn't stifle a small smile at seeing Andrew surreptitiously adding a shot of whisky to his own and Simon's cups from a pocket flask. She relaxed gratefully into Simon's hold as a creeping weariness made its way from her aching head slowly down to her swollen tired feet. Helen had no notion of her eyes sliding shut until Simon lifted her into his arms and announced he was taking her up to bed.

Tenderly sliding off her shoes he rubbed the blood back into circulation. She lay utterly passive allowing him to slowly peel off her clothes and pull a soft clean nightdress down over her shivering skin. The evening was drawing in, papered by a silvery drizzle, and a faint pink sunset shimmered in the stormy sky. As he closed the curtains Simon's body was silhouetted against the pale light and overwhelming love swept through Helen. Her words were barely audible but he had no trouble hearing them. 'Lay down with me until I sleep. Please.'

Simon slid into the bed, cupping her from behind and sending his comfort through her veins. He was lulled by a combination of relief and whisky into a light sleep as faint voices drifted up the stairs.

Andrew Campbell hesitated, unsure how to answer James's question as to whether things were okay. It was a blessing the man had already been well on his way when they'd called him – James hadn't been able to forget what had happened the last time he'd ignored his instincts. The question still had to be answered and although the word okay had a connotation he wasn't sure applied but everything was relative and considering recent events it could be worse so he nodded reluctant agreement.

James knelt by Paul's side to check his pulse. The hand hung loose and pale with the fingers trailing on the carpet. 'Get some water please.' He dampened Paul's cracked lips. His partner's stressed body heaved with dry coughs and James moved his hands to Paul's shoulders staying his effort to sit up. It didn't stop his wild unfocused eyes from searching the room.

Andrew observed the younger doctor's kindness to the man who'd sometimes mocked him, his soothing touch and murmuring words allowed Paul's taut limbs to sink into sorely needed rest. The monotonous tone of the quietly ticking mantelpiece clock lulled for a while until footsteps echoed on the bare wood stairs.

CHAPTER THIRTY-TWO

'Love does not begin and end the way we seem to think it does. Love is a battle, love is a war; love is a growing up.'
James Baldwin

'I'm starving, how about...'

The words died on Simon's tongue as his eyes met Andrew Campbell's warning glance. All his father could do was trust that he'd taught the boy well. Though not born of his blood no birth son could be more like him. He had to rely on that.

Simon walked steadily across the room to sit down next to Paul giving no hint that he recognized the fact that the others were all collectively holding their breath. As he often did he used the benefit of habitual patience to wait for Paul to speak first. It's plainly a struggle for him to put any words together that make sense.

'Is Helen all right?' A mixture of love and fierce protection flashes across Simon's face burning through his answer, 'She's sleeping right now. She'll be fine.' Paul has no choice but to turn away, his hands clutching a pillow in front of him for security like a small child. The sight of his son's nakedly open feelings is almost too much for him to stand.

'If you all wouldn't mind I'd like to speak to Paul alone please.' The only help Andrew can provide is to stop Margaret's protest with a tight handclasp.

'Can I get you a drink Paul?'

It wasn't a wise thing to offer but he hadn't known where to start. As the tension eases from Paul's face it brings back more of the look of the man Simon had first met. His voice comes out as steady, betraying no hint of the longing ripping him up inside. 'No thanks. I don't think that's a good idea.'

His rueful smile so eerily resembles the one Simon sees reflected back every morning in the mirror that it dissolves his resolve to remain unapologetic. Without any real thought he takes Paul's cold clammy hands in his own warm ones and speaks probably the first totally honest words between them. 'I'm sorry for everything.' Such pointless words in many ways – not enough and yet too much.

Paul's eyes were full to the brim of tears and his reply far from what Simon expected or felt he deserved. 'It's all right. Really.' The simple forgiveness was humbling and freed Simon to say the other things he desperately needed to get out. Without that he was

232

never going to be able to move on. 'I meant to stop when I'd hurt you enough but...'

There is no justification a man can decently use, to excuse falling in love with someone else's wife. They were both more than old enough to know that. 'I tried to stay away but I couldn't leave her be. I know I did wrong but...' Simon's knuckles flexed white as chalk dust, 'I can't forget what you did to Helen and our baby. I really am trying to forgive, for my own sake as well as yours, but it's hard. Of course you probably want to smash my face in too which just maybe brings us somewhere close to even.' A reluctant parental pride at his son's honesty brought the faintest sliver of a smile to Paul's face.

'Go ahead and hit me if it helps. It'll make no difference because I've discovered these last few months...' He swallowed hard as the words almost choked in his throat. 'Nothing can stop me loving you and believe me I've tried. Penalty of fatherhood I guess.' Tentatively he reached over and risked stroking the crown of Simon's bent head. The volume of Paul's words dropped to an almost inaudible sigh. 'I still love Helen terribly and the only grain of consolation I've been able to find is that in a way she's fallen in love with a better part of me.'

His shaking fingers ran through the lose strands of Simon's glossy black hair while his mind struggled to picture what his baby son must have been like. Paul's heart flooded with sadness at all he'd missed because of youthful foolishness. Picturing Simon as a sturdy little boy toddling around, sitting on another man's lap and calling him Daddy – that pierced his heart worse than any knife.

Simon had been wrong on that first visit because Paul had never banished him from his thoughts – not for one solitary day. If he hadn't stupidly kept secrets from Helen they might have found Simon together and... That was a direction he didn't dare to go in.

Something worthwhile had to be dragged from this mess but Paul had no clue what it might be. It had felt like being on a torture rack earlier to be forced to watch them place their hands jointly on Helen's stomach checking the safety of their child.

'Paul? Paul are you all right?'

'Yes of course.' It was up to him to be convincing. This was a small thing to do for his son – some measure of reparation for all the other times when he'd failed him. Suddenly a tired longing for home enveloped his body. Marion's quiet personality seemed terribly appealing. Her self-containment demanded little – a welcome contrast to Helen's draining emotional neediness. Unable to visualize it before, Paul could now clearly see a life with her as one of welcome steadiness with no mountains and valleys of feeling. It was the only way he would be able to survive.

'Simon, I must be leaving now.' Standing he cleared his throat awkwardly searching yet again for the right thing to say. While he tried Simon stared directly into Paul's shadowed eyes and held out his hand. Hesitantly Paul took it, only softly at first, afraid it might be snatched away again. Simon had no idea before he did it what his next move would be surprising them both as he opened his arms wide and pulled his father into an embrace neither had expected.

For the first time Paul held his son.

The warmth of him, the meeting of bone to bone, the mutual tears, was the most powerful thing he'd ever experienced. It took every atom of strength to move away knowing he might never be given this chance again. Once in thirty years wasn't enough.

'Call when you're able and good luck with...' Paul couldn't finish – he wasn't quite that courageous. Calling to James and polite goodbyes to the Campbells glossed over the farewells neither could say.

After the retreating car lights were swallowed up by the velvety darkness Simon turned the lights off and locked the door before walking slowly upstairs. Helen slept heavily, her soft hair spread over the pillow, the curve of her mouth barely visible in the glow of the bedside light. Dropping his clothes in an untidy heap on the carpet he slipped quietly, under the covers. She moved slightly onto her side as Simon slid an arm underneath to pull her close, needing her comfort this night. He dampened the selfishness that made him long to wake her and instead lay quietly until the sun began its inexorable rise.

They had another day. That was really all anyone could hope for.

EPILOGUE

The Fraserburgh Guardian –
14 February 2002

Helen and Simon Campbell of Montrace announce with pleasure the birth of their daughter Kirsty Margaret. Great-grandmother Alice Barton, grandparents Mary and Henry Trewarren, Margaret and Andrew Campbell, Marion and Paul Barton all welcome her into the world with love.

The East Cornwall Courier –
11 October 2002

Marion and Paul Barton of St. Within announce with pleasure the birth of their son William Jack. Grandmothers Betty Walden and Alice Barton, brother and sister-in-law Simon and Helen Campbell all welcome him into the world with love.

Alice sticks the announcements proudly in her new album. A photograph of Kirsty wearing the Campbell family christening gown shows jet-black hair under her lace

237

cap setting off her startling emerald green eyes and clear skin. In another, the camera catches William last month at his own christening, in white silk shorts and shirt, his bright blue eyes sparkling in his thin lightly freckled face. This would have made Jack so happy.

Marion comes in with the tea tray so Alice sighs quietly to herself and puts the book away. She's mustn't dawdle. The household revolves around baby William now. Alice has got what she asked for.

The publishers hope that this book has given you enjoyable reading. Large Print Books are especially designed to be as easy to see and hold as possible. If you wish a complete list of our books please ask at your local library or write directly to:

Dales Large Print Books
Magna House, Long Preston,
Skipton, North Yorkshire.
BD23 4ND

This Large Print Book, for people
who cannot read normal print,
is published under the auspices of

THE ULVERSCROFT FOUNDATION